A Melancholy Event

Dan Glaister

unbound

This edition first published in 2021

Unbound
6th Floor Mutual House, 70 Conduit Street, London W1S 2GF
www.unbound.com

ISBN (eBook): 978-1-78965-122-5
ISBN (Paperback): 978-1-78965-121-8

Cover design by Mecob

Printed and bound in Great Britain by Clays Ltd, Elcograf S.p.A.

About the Author

Dan Glaister was born and grew up in the south of England, going on to work at the *Guardian* as a writer, editor and foreign correspondent. He is captivated by the stories embedded in the landscape, by the traces they leave and how they seep into our present. He lives in Gloucestershire, near the setting of this, his first novel.

Super Patrons

Sarah Akure Wall
Jackie Anthoney
Neil Arthur
Katie Baker
Stephen Baker
John Baxter
Hillary Bedell
Dan Berkson
Peter Black
Derek Brewer
Ken Brickley
Michaela Carmichael
David Corio
Geoff Cox
Valentine Cunningham
Adrian Currie
Victoria Dailey
Klare Davis
Jenny Dempsey
Tom Dixon
Esmee Ducasse

David Entwistle
Sarah Entwistle
Richard Eyre
Andrew Gilchrist
Andrew Glaister
Gabrielle Glaister
Lalage Glaister
Paul Glaister
Jonathan Glancey
Eileen Graham
Jules Graham
Lucy Gray
Joanna Greenhill Holland
Arthur Hamlyn
Peggy Harbord
David Hardwick
Alex Haye
Christina Heward-Mills
Charlotte Higgins
Anya Hughes
Debbie Innes-Turnill
Joan Irvine
Sylvia Jessop
Evelyn Jones
Ali Kayley
Val Kayley
William Kayley
Martin Kettle
Naseem Khan
Helen Kincaid
Pete Kitson
Nathan Lake
Maya Law

Jonny Leck
Linda McLemore
Carla Mendonca
Philip Middleton
Carol Morris
Richard Morris
Lynn Morss
Simon Nelson
Mandy Oudhuis
D Pitt
Jane Quinn
Thibaut Remoundos
Ada Rice
The Seftons
Richard Shea
Paul Sheppard
Charmian Skinner
Tony Thorne
Tamsin Treverton Jones
Renee Vargas
Cindy Wall
Ed Wall
Dale Warren
Lola Watkins
Paul Webster
Nicole Weerman
Howard Wilkie
Rebecca Winton
Theresa Witziers
Amy Woodrow
Brian Wynn
Terri Young

The Story

Stephanie found the story that would end her life in a cardboard box in the attic. 'Do not remove,' it said in felt-tip pen on the top of the box. Inside were deeds, square yards of parchment inscribed with the scrawl of age, deeds unknown and undreamt of, deeds binding souls long passed, wills and probates, testaments and tenancies. Among them, within the permissions and remissions, folded on a fragile piece of lined paper so worn that its creases had become cuts, was the story.

Stephanie wasn't usually one for stories. 'Stephanie doesn't much care for literature,' her mother would pronounce.

'I can't be bothered,' she'd correct her. 'What's the point? All those words, it takes too long. They're not real. I'd rather be doing things.'

What those things might be Stephanie never really knew, but she was sure they were better than reading, having her head lodged between the pages of a book, like her brother. He was doing it now, in the living room with the lamp on and the curtains drawn, wasting summer. He would be in the armchair by the window, staring at the words, unaware of which part of his anatomy his hand was scratching – his nose, his ear, his

1

bottom – the hand only breaking its monotony of irritation to turn the page, lips exhaling the words.

She could see him even though she was two floors up in the attic, looking down on it all. The attic was her most recent place, hers until her brother eventually found her there and told her mother and then she would need somewhere else. But for the time being it was hers, away from being part of them.

The story in her hands covered two sides of mottled paper decorated with the precise slanting hand of another age. In places the letters were illegible, the words unlikely or unknown, the writing too stylised to be decipherable. The date, however, was clear, even though the ones looked like sevens: 1807.

Kneeling in the dust and debris of the attic with the paper unfolded before her, Stephanie read the story from 170 years before. The creases in the paper formed a grid, the neat rhythm of the script intersected and disrupted by the marks of the fold. She leaned forward to follow the story in the half-light from the window set high up in the gable end of the house. She read the words: *A melancholy event.*

These would be her words. She was the one who had found them, the one who had opened the box and taken the fragile paper in hand.

August 14, 1807. Duel between Lieut Benjamin Heazle, 3rd Regt or Old Buffs & Lieut Joseph Francis Delmont, 82nd Regt. Second, Lieut John Sargeaunt, 61st Regt.

'Duel.' She wasn't sure if she'd said the word out loud or just to herself. 'Duel.' She said it again, aloud this time, tasting it, feeling the two vowels roll around each other in her mouth. Images of pistols and sabres, cowboys and gentlemen rushed into her mind, dropped handkerchiefs and top hats, ladies swooning beneath spreading oak trees as the best of society sacrificed itself to honour.

Stephanie knew about honour. After her father had left there had been many muttered conversations about honour. The grown-ups, many of whom she did not know, took to whispering urgently only to fall quiet when they sensed her presence. She heard enough to know that they were more concerned with an absence of honour than with its presence. Their silences, the furtive glances in her direction, suggested that she was the one who had brought dishonour to the family, that it was she who had driven her father away.

She said the word again: 'Duel.' What better way to redress a wrong, to reclaim honour?

Since her father had departed there had been nothing for her; she had become a stray note in the harmonious accord of her mother and brother. Her mother barely seemed to recognise her now, Stephanie's presence eliciting little more than a dim acknowledgement, an acceptance on her mother's part that this figure had a place – although she was unable to recall precisely what that place might be.

She felt the paper between her fingers, its crisp finish softened with age. In one section the writing had turned brown, the lead grey of the ink bleached by whatever light or chemical had reached inside the box to fall upon the uppermost quadrant of the four-folded sheet.

Delmont and Heazle. Stephanie knew these names. She lived in Delmont Lane. Beyond that was Heazle Place, a dead end of once-new houses positioned in a crescent by a post-war planner with a zeal for symmetry.

Delmont a good–looking man, open agreeable countenance age 22. Heazle a native of Bandon, near Cork, tall, strong–built man. Swarthy complexion, 28 years old.

She would challenge her brother to a duel. She would reclaim her honour. Wrongs would be set right, and the long summer that lay ahead would pass.

But who would she be? She sat back, off her knees, seeing the two men. They both had uniforms, but she couldn't quite decide how the uniforms should be. Would they have been redcoats, with muskets and funny black hats like stovepipes? Or would it have been more drab, grey and blue with long, heavy woollen coats rather than jackets? Stephanie stood up, put her shoulders back and puffed up her chest. She was a tall strong man. She pushed her chin out but it was no good. She was too fair, her face still flecked with the freckles of childhood, mouse-blonde hair shooing away any notion of a swarthy complexion. Good looking and agreeable was what she would be. She changed attitude, relaxing her body, legs apart, hand on hip, like a picture of a Georgian gentleman. She would be Delmont, the one who died.

The brother would be Heazle, the murderer. She sat back, pleased with herself. Her brother would kill her. He was so wrapped up in his book, so oblivious to anything beyond the page in front of him, that he wouldn't realise until it was too late. Then he would be judged, he would feel the force of injustice.

The Grange stands on the Western side of a small dell, which running up from the valley into the body of Wickeridge Hill, terminates near the road from Beeches Green to the Grange, becomes in passing that place, a steep hollow lane, leading down across the dell on its way to the South side of the hill. The field selected for the duel, lies in this dell, about 120 yards above the place where the lane crosses it.

Her fingers ran right to left, down to up across the paper as if following the lines of a map, tracing a route. She knew those fields, knew that track. Her mind passed through the field to the edge of the woods, the steep valley wall pitching down to the brook below.

The old orchard by the brook was one of her places too, somewhere she'd go to be quiet, to be away on her own. She'd climb the apple trees, perching a few feet off the ground as if seeking shelter from an impending flood, enjoying the pain of the trees' gnarled limbs pressing into her flesh. In the autumn, when there would be fruit in the trees, she'd lie on a branch and watch the sky through the leaves, letting her eyes fall out of focus so that the precise red orbs would bleed across the green of the foliage, streaking the sky.

Stephanie was at that age in her teens when she was neither in one world nor the other. Her face had not been described as pretty. The mouth was too thin, the jaw too angular, the head too small. The shape of it all, an inverted isosceles triangle with the chin at its point, a chin that would turn red at moments of anger or excitement, held a certain vulnerability, a fragility that might suggest a sensitive disposition. This, however, was misleading, for Stephanie prided herself on a lack of sentiment. She found herself surrounded by sentimentality of the worst kind, the cloying bonhomie of family embracing her, suffocating her. She had determined that before she had finished with her childhood she would set herself apart from that sentiment. So she had become what she was: a girl not yet woman who was different, different to the other girls, different to the boys, different to the other members of her family. She wore jeans not skirts, rode bikes not ponies, left her long hair tangled and unbrushed. Her eyes, which might have been considered her most arresting feature, possessing a cool, grey detachment, betrayed nothing, neither fear nor happiness. They were, effectively, dead. This pleased Stephanie. She had heard about windows into the soul and decided that hers should remain closed, shut to all. Her eyes would be a mask, a protective screen.

Once she had set upon that course, the rest had been simple. People did not look into her, for they could not see. Or if they did look, they saw themselves and quickly moved on. Some, of course, found this alluring.

Duel fought with old horse-pistols – Delmont's was rusty. Duellists placed back to back & made to walk six paces.

She could feel his back pressed into hers, his strong built back against her, tense, alert. They were in white shirts now, their uniforms gathered together in a bundle by the second, Sargeaunt, clumped under a tree, readied for a return, to be donned and filled and stuffed with living bodies. Now she hears Sargeaunt, his voice high in the summer evening air, spiralling up and up as he sings his ritual: back to back, six paces, stop and turn, shoot on command. These are the rules.

Delmont was shot in the left side before as he turned was turning to receive his opponent's fire. Bullet also wounded his left arm & came out at the chest.

Stephanie fell, her side burning, gripped by fire, her left arm inert by her side. She writhed on the floor of the attic, feeling the blood pool around her.

Delmont buried in S.W. corner of the burial ground of the parish Church. Flat Stone 'Here lie remains of Lieut J... F... D... of HM 82 Regt born November 25, 1785, died August 18, 1807.

She lay panting on the floor, the window looking down at her. She would be Delmont. That much was clear. And the brother would be Heazle. He would argue, say it wasn't fair, but she was always able to make him do what she wanted.

The Recruit

He was in the chair by the window, scratching. It made her itch.

'Look what I found.' She made her voice bright but he didn't hear. Head bowed, lips moving.

'Look!' She held out the papers. His lips carried on moving but he raised his head, eyes vacant behind the glasses, the hand settling on the open book, index finger extended to mark a point on the page.

'Pieces of paper.' He shrugged. Matthew was older than Stephanie, but only in years. His friends' parents, if he had visited one of their houses, would struggle to remember which one he had been: the plain one, the one with glasses, the one with the parting. His blandness was infuriating to Stephanie, who found herself unable to reconcile it with his superior position in the family.

'They're old,' she said. 'More than a hundred years old. It's a story about a duel.'

The hand rested on the book; again the head came up.

'So?'

'It was here.'

'What do you mean here?'

'In the fields. Look.' She held up the piece of paper again, as if it were a picture of the place, as if he would see it just by looking. 'Delmont,' she said. 'That was his name. And the other one was Heazle.'

He took the piece of paper she proffered, his head bowed to it and his hand idly began to scratch behind his ear. She slapped his hand.

'What did you do that for?'

'You were scratching. Mother says you shouldn't.'

He turned his head back to the paper, its edge trembling in his hand.

'I think we should do it.' She swallowed. There. She had said it.

He didn't look up. She slapped him again, playfully.

'What?' Now he looked at her.

'We should have a duel, like they did.'

'Why?'

'Because it's there. Because it's meant for us. You can be Heazle.'

He glanced again at the paper. 'I don't want to be Heazle. Why do I have to be Heazle?'

For a moment she thought she would be pitying, but she settled instead on cold.

'Because you do. I can't be Heazle. I have to be Delmont, the good-looking one. The one who dies.'

She took back the paper and pushed him outside then, through the door and into the garden, propelling him before her like a prisoner, pinning his arms to his sides. The wind was blowing, a warm breeze propelling flat clouds high through the sky. She positioned him in the centre of the lawn, standing upright, to attention.

'Doesn't work,' she said. The rotating whirligig of the washing line was in the way.

'Help me move this.' She was already pulling at it, bending down to heave at its base as if trying to uproot a tree. 'Matthew!'

He stirred from his position and stepped towards her.

'Here,' he said, placing a hand on the shaft of the line and lifting it up. 'Where shall I put it?'

'I don't know. Anywhere.'

Matthew looked around him and placed the washing line neatly alongside the flowerbed. He looked at his sister.

'What are we doing?'

'The duel,' she said. She brushed her hair away from her face, but it blew back, covering her eyes, getting in her mouth. She took his arms again, pinning them to his sides, and walked him backwards to where he had been.

'Stay there.' She walked around him and stood with her back to him, moving until she felt the jut of his bony shoulder blades.

'Six paces,' she said, her voice rising, 'then we turn.' She brushed her hair away again, wishing she had tied it back. She could feel the blood moving through her body, the pulse of it. Above her, two crows harried a kestrel, the smaller bird flying on serenely while the larger black shapes sniped at it, screeching as they flitted above and beneath their quarry.

She took a breath.

Then she counted.

'One!' Her voice felt small in the breeze.

'Two.' It was as if she was walking on a tightrope or a ledge, her balance deserting her. She put her arms out to steady herself even though she knew this was wrong.

'Three.' The kestrel was still there, the crows attendant to it.

'Four.'

'Five.' The kestrel had disappeared from her view.

'Six.' She took the pace and stopped. Should she turn? Should she say to turn? She turned and looked up, almost flinching at the expectation stirring in her.

Matthew was staring at her, standing in the spot where she had left him, where they had stood back to back.

'What are you doing there?' she shouted. 'You were supposed to move, to do the paces like me.' She felt dizzy, and sat down where she was, as if struck.

'I thought that was what he did,' Matthew said. 'Just turned around and shot without doing the paces.' Matthew shrugged. 'So that's what I did.'

'You're useless, Matthew.' She stood up and ran at him, pushing her hands into him, knocking him back, winding him. 'You – Heazle – take the steps, the paces, but then you turn around before the last one and shoot Delmont – me – before I can raise my gun. Idiot.'

She was over him now, Matthew kneeling on the ground, puffing his cheeks out while she paced around in front of him, arms flailing, hair whipping across her face.

'And then, as I turn, as I start to turn, you shoot me, through the side, like in the story, through my arms and into my chest, and I fall, maybe I stagger and then I fall, like this.' She threw herself to the ground, clawing at the grass with her fingers, body twitching while Matthew knelt beside her, doing his best to ignore his sister.

'I'm going back in,' he said. He started to rise, but she grabbed his arm.

'I'm not mad.' She used her quiet voice, like the stern one their mother would use to make them believe that she was really furious, although she was the only one who ended up believing it.

Matthew looked at her, looked at her hand on his arm, the nails bitten back, ragged and dirty.

'I'm going back to my book,' he told her.

'You're scared.'

He turned and walked slowly back towards the house. Stephanie looked around for something to throw at him, a stone, even the washing line, but there was nothing. She watched him tread deliberate steps across the grass and down to the house.

'Where can I get a gun?' she called out. He stopped.

'You could ask Mr Birch. He's got a gun.'

'He'd never lend it to me,' she replied. 'He loves his gun almost as much as his dog.'

She followed him as he went into the house. Mother was waiting for them. 'You two seem to be having a nice time. It looked like you were playing blind man's buff, except you didn't have a blindfold.' She paused, a polite, enquiring smile on her face. Stephanie always thought that her mother was playing the part of a mother in a drama, with everything arranged, every nuanced gesture speaking of something else.

'Darling?'

'We were having a duel,' said Matthew. 'Steph found a duel, well, the story of an old duel across the valley and she wanted to act it out.'

'Matthew, shut up,' said Stephanie.

'That sounds exciting, dear,' said her mother. 'Where did you find the story? I hope nobody died.'

Stephanie looked at her mother. She was neither tall nor short, fat nor thin, and wore her dark hair in such a conventional style that the whole assemblage had often caused Stephanie, in her early childhood, to fail to recognise her, to run up to a female figure of a certain age in a supermarket or on the high street and grasp her only to find that it was someone else, someone unknown.

'I don't really want to talk about it,' Stephanie said. 'It's just a story. I don't even know if it's true.'

'You should investigate, it might give you something nice to do for the summer, something fulfilling,' her mother said.

'How do I do that?'

Her mother pretended she was giving the question consideration. 'Well, you could try the library,' she said. 'I'm sure they have records of local events. Do be careful though, duelling can be very dangerous.'

She turned to Matthew. 'Now, darling, tell me, where are you with the book? Did you get to the end of the chapter?' Her mother, it seemed, had exhausted the subject of the duel and had reverted to the more familiar terrain of her brother's reading, using their private language, a code Stephanie had not been given. Stephanie watched them, hearing the noise of their words. Her mother was animated, her face bright like the grown-ups Stephanie had watched at the parties her parents used to throw when her father had been there, noisy affairs full of shrieking and laughter, her mother being too loud, cigarette in hand, gushing over people she barely knew while her father moved through the house being far too nice to everybody.

'Why do I need to be careful?' She asked the question quietly, voicing the thought that had been welling inside her. The two did not interrupt their conversation to answer her. She said it again, more strident: 'Why do I need to be careful?'

The Reward

It wasn't the first time she'd been to the library in town. It was, though, the first time she had been to the library unaccompanied, of her own volition. In spite of this landmark, the man behind the window in the lobby seemed unimpressed. He did the bookish thing that the brother did, not looking up, not seeing Stephanie until she was close enough to smell his air of decay.

She repeated her sentence, the sentence she'd practised at home, first with hushed reverence, then helplessness, before settling on politeness laced with urgency.

'I need to find some information about a melancholy event that took place in 1807,' she pronounced to the top of the man's head. The head rotated slowly on the neck and a once-thin face came into view. What might have been angular was jowly, the skin grey beneath a pair of black-framed glasses, dark hair falling in a lank parting.

'Local newspaper records are through the door to the right,' he said in a monotone, as if reading a script, eyes moving to his left. His teeth were yellow and crooked. The head pivoted back down to the desk. Stephanie looked around her. The library had only been built a few years before, a replacement for the grand stone building in the middle of the town, a place of polished banisters and creaking floorboards. The new library, a squat, greying structure already showing its age, was on a side street behind a church. There was a fleeting sense to the interior, as if it might easily be dismantled from one day to the next and turned to another use or replaced with something more tangible, more permanent.

To Stephanie's right there were two identical doors. She turned to the desk to ask the man which one she should use but he had gone, leaving a trail of pencils, scissors and a neat stack of blue library cards. She looked behind her. There was no one else in the lobby. Stephanie leaned over the counter and took one of the cards, sliding it into the back pocket of her jeans with a practised movement. She reached back and took a pencil as well, an important item, she now realised, that she had forgotten to bring with her.

She chose the door on the left. Inside was a small room, white ceiling tiles bearing a line of neon lights encased in wire cages. In front of her was another counter with a window. The man from the lobby sat behind the glass, his head bent down as he busied himself rearranging library cards. As the door swung shut behind Stephanie he looked up and smiled at her.

'Hello, good morning. How can I help you?'

Stephanie stared at him. She was sure he was the same man, with the same hair and the same glasses, but his voice was different, as different as his manner. He sat there beaming at her, his smile unwavering. Stephanie stared at his teeth. For a moment she struggled to remember the phrase she had learned. 'Mysterious event?' 'Momentous event?' She could feel a flush spreading up her chin. Finally it came to her.

'I need to find some information about a melancholy event that took place in 1807,' she said, urgent but polite.

'1807,' the man repeated back to her. 'That would be in the

16

local newspaper records.' He bared his teeth at Stephanie. She tried to smile back but it was hard.

'Can I see them, please?' Stephanie tried her absolute hardest to use her most polite voice, the voice she almost never used.

'Yes, of course,' said the man. He picked up a card and held a pen over it. 'Now, what date were you interested in?'

Stephanie wanted to say that she had just told him, but she was worried that might be breaking the rules of this game that she did not understand.

'1807,' she said.

'Yes,' the man said, his smile faltering, 'but what date in 1807?'

Stephanie felt tired.

'Date,' she said. 'August, August the fourteenth.'

The man bent his head down again to write on one of the cards. She watched his writing sprawl along the faint lines. Upside down, she noticed, the writing was similar to the writing on the sheet of paper she had found in the attic.

'A melancholy event,' he wrote. 'August 14, 1807.' The ones looked like sevens.

'Name?' He paused, his head down, his hand held above the paper. Stephanie could see the end of his pencil quivering, the slightest tremble as he waited, the moment suspended.

'Name?' He looked up, the smile taking shape on his mouth as he raised his face, the hand still poised over the card. Her mind raced, through the door, out on to the street, back to the house and up the stairs, into the attic.

'Delmont,' she said.

The librarian looked up at Stephanie, his eyes travelling over her blue jeans, her faded T-shirt with its picture of a cartoon mouse, her green parka with the furry hood held in front of her. His hand reached forward. In it was the small blue index card with the curly writing.

'Out of the door, turn left and go through the door,' he said. 'The materials will be brought to you.' He stood, hands by his sides, waiting for Stephanie. She nodded, not knowing what to say, and turned to go, the lines of carpet tiles running across and away from her. By habit she did not step on the lines, not wanting to disturb the dead. As she walked she straightened her back, imagining herself the young recruit, proud of his regiment.

The lobby was still empty, the window slid shut now across the desk where the librarian had been sitting. She pushed at the door to her left and found herself in another plain room, two metal tables set end to end, their white tops empty, blue plastic chairs tucked under. The librarian entered bearing a cardboard box before him, like the boxes that used to contain her father's new shirts.

'A melancholy event,' he said, setting it down on the table in front of Stephanie. She wished she hadn't used the phrase, or that she had said it in a different tone, that she had made it sound light hearted, as if its tragedy could only be comic.

Stephanie looked at the box, grey and rigid with a strap to hold it shut. It smelled of dust and the past, like the box in the attic. Inside were a few sheets of paper, mainly cuttings from newspapers stuck on to card, the paper flaking with age, fragments of parchment scattered across the bottom of the box, like flakes of dead skin.

One piece of paper was slightly larger than the others, the paper still robust despite its age. Stephanie took it between her thin fingers.

MURDER!!

The word was at the top of the page, the biggest word on the piece of paper, looming over all that came below. She felt a rush of dizziness as she realised that the story of the duel was true, that the paper she held under the bright lights of the library was calling to her from the past.

FORTY GUINEAS REWARD.

She wanted to laugh but stopped herself, aware that it wasn't done to laugh in libraries. Her brother would be a murderer, a price on his head. She would be the injured party. Instead of looking at her accusingly, people would regard her with sympathy. Like her, they would wonder whether there was any justice in the world.

The paper was pocked with marks of damp, its seemingly random arrangement of capitals and lower case, italic and bold lending it the appearance of something that might have been thrown together with a child's printing set. Stephanie leaned forward to read the poster, tipping the metal chair on to its front two legs. The reward offered was 20 guineas each for Heazle and Sargeaunt, charged with,

the wilful Murder of Lieutenant JOSEPH FRANCIS DELMONT.

Both had,

absconded and fled from Juſtice.

Stephanie listened to the throbbing inside her head. The only other sound in the room came from the overhead light, a faint buzzing that lowered in tone each time the light flickered.

THE above named BENJAMIN HEAZLE is ſtrong built, about 28 years of age, 5 feet 10 or 11 inches high, dark swarthy Complexion, black Eyes, very dark short brown Hair, and is a Native of Bandon near Cork in Ireland; HAD on when he absconded, a very dark Cotie

*cut very full in front, or frock fashion, a striped toillenet Waistcoat, blue
cloth Pantaloons, long military Boots, a black beaver Hat, bent both
before and behind, which nearly covered half of his face, lisps a little,
and has the Irish accent very strongly in conversation.*

She sat back, her lips moving as she tried to mimic a strong
Irish accent. Visions of the dashing soldier fleeing the town
coursed through her mind, his hat pulled low over his face.
She lisped a few words, feeling them play along her lips, before
remembering where she was.

She turned back to the poster before her, and began to
read about the second, a 'well-built, handsome Man, about 26
years of Age', with a dark complexion and black eyes. She
liked Sargeaunt more than Heazle; his black eyes pierced her,
making her shudder.

*HAD on when he absconded, a dark fashionable corbeau Coat, with
white metal Buttons, a buff cassimere Waistcoat, light drab colored
worsted Pantaloons, military half Boots, a black beaver Hat, wide in
the brim, and has a pleasing address.*

At the bottom of the poster, written in a thin spidery scrawl
was a message:

The particulars of this case are written on the back of this handbill.

She turned the paper over to find that the spider had spread
across the entire sheet, leaving an elegant trail of curlicues and
ink-stained footprints. Delmont, Heazel and Sargeaunt, the
spider told her, were recruiting officers based in the town.

*On Friday 14th August Delmont and Heazle after dining together
went out for a walk Delmont used some expressions, which Heazle
took as an insult, and demanded an apology, which Delmont refused,
and they agreed to meet and settle the matter in the evening. Delmont*

sent for Sargeaunt to come and meet them. He was unable to reconcile them and went and procured pistols and accompanied the two others to a field near the Grange. Delmont was shot through the body…

Stephanie felt her side, the air rushing out of her, and watched as the handwriting writhed across the paper, alive, pulling her down. She woke with a start, just able to regain her balance before the chair fell and tipped her to the floor. Delmont had been taken to his lodgings in a scallet, a hand barrow procured from a nearby dyehouse. The author of the scrawl had added a riddle:

When antecryst is come in to this world, what thynge shall be hardest to him to knowe? A hand-barrowe, for of that he shall not knowe which ende shall goo before.

The hand barrow was covered with cushions obtained from the Grange before Delmont was taken to the town.

He languished until the following Thursday and then expired. Before his death he said that he and Heazle were placed back to back and ordered to retire six paces and then turn around & fire, that he was shot in the back before he had completed his sixth pace and before he had turned around to receive his adversary's fire, that the word 'fire' was not given – Heazle and Sargeaunt both absconded – They were advertised in the Provincial papers but without success.

Holding her breath, Stephanie picked up the poster, folded it carefully and stuffed it into her pocket. She was fearful that the librarian would be waiting for her in the lobby, but again the window was closed and she bolted through the door and into the street.

The Soldier

Stephanie stopped running. Her father had taken her here, marvelling at the sweep of the hill as it cascaded down the valley, gesturing with his arms as if he owned it, as if this was his work. Her young eyes had been too innocent to see anything but a view, nothing but fields and hedges and trees. Now she fell on the grass, her heart pounding, tongue thick in her mouth, the land around her still, waiting. She took the reward poster from the back pocket of her jeans and gazed at the fragment of another time. One corner of the paper was dotted with mould, pale brown spots spreading across the paper like a rash.

MURDER!!

She walked home, dreaming as she idled along the lane. How much had changed since the duel? Cars rarely came up the lane, the tarmac giving way to a dirt track, a rutted carriageway that meandered along the ridgeline before narrowing to little more than a bridleway as it descended the far side of the hill. She envisaged Heazle and Delmont walking that same path, their spirits tinged by the quiet majesty of the landscape.

The house stood on the side of a hill at the edge of the town, rows of dwellings snaking into the distance before dipping out of view, the town itself shrouded by the surrounding valleys.

Even in summer the house was in a state of perpetual gloom, its small windows refusing to admit more than a glimmer of light. Stephanie marvelled at the way the aged glass warped whatever light did penetrate, throwing patterns on the walls. She would try to talk to her parents about what was in the patterns, explain to them that there was more in the house than they knew, but they were never interested.

Now that there were just the three of them, they seemed to live in shadow. Light bulbs blew and were left abandoned in their fittings. Her mother said it was because the wiring was old and the whole place needed fixing, but she had never done anything about it, saying that it was too much for them to manage, and that anyway they were fine as they were. Even Matthew protested, his nose dipping ever closer to his book.

She remembered how the house had felt like a museum when they had moved in, the damp and dust heavy in the air, as if the door had not been opened for years. The previous owners had seemed to simply get up one day and go, leaving most of their furniture behind: heavy wooden chairs, beds with mattresses stuffed with horse hair, big chairs with gold tassels, a solid chest of drawers that would have been impossible to get down the stairs and could only have been brought up in pieces to be assembled in the bedroom where it now stood. There were even a few pictures on the walls, a painting of a sailing ship off the coast of a tropical island, small figures playing on the shoreline. Stephanie would stare at the painting uncomprehending. What might they be doing there? Was it always summer in that faraway place? Might this be where

Heazle had fled? She imagined him in this strange land, sweat running down his face as he struggled to walk along the beach under the weight of his thick woollen coat. She would lose herself in the landscape, feeling the sand warm the soles of her feet, the sea soft on her toes. She could never understand what such a carefree, warm scene was doing on the walls of this dark house.

She went to the kitchen and took a pair of scissors from the drawer. She was sure now. She took them up to the attic, pulling the metal steps up behind her, like a drawbridge.

She stood in the still light, chest heaving, and pulled the blade of the scissors across her hand, like a barber with a razor, feeling the grain of the metal across her skin, watching the flush of pink it left on her palm. She set a mirror on the ledge in front of her. The light from the window cast a pale hue across her face. How should it be, this haircut that would last forever? She had seldom if ever cut her hair. On a few occasions her mother had taken her to the hairdressers before the beginning of the school year, but Stephanie had protested so much that she had not persisted. After that her hair had simply grown, long and untrained, down her back, growing faster than she herself did, as if it was racing to the ground before it was out of reach.

The scissors were sturdy, suited more to flesh than fabric. She fitted the loops of the handles over the fingers of her right hand, two thin fingers through the larger of the two, the thumb hooked into the smaller loop. She took a bunch of hair in her left hand. She looked at herself in the mirror, expectant, a speck of fear in her eyes. She made herself watch, not following the operation of her hands but staring instead at herself, staring into her own eyes, registering alarm and rebellion.

The first cut that Stephanie made at her hair was not clean, the scissors struggling to shear through so much material. She pulled her hand away, leaving strands of hair dangling, half hewn, her head lopsided.

It made her laugh, and seeing her laughter in the mirror made her laugh more still. She felt dizzy, weightless, as if the cutting of her hair had unbalanced her, like a cat that had lost its whiskers. Never cut a cat's whiskers. When Stephanie had tried it, enticing a cat with some food, stroking it, running her hand the length of its arched back, feeling the tiny frame respond to the sweep of her hand, when she had held its head in her hand, held it tightly, felt its fragility, realised that she could crush it merely by squeezing her hand tighter, then banished that awareness, when she had brought the scissors to its face and cut, there had been nothing. The cat watched her, as she now watched herself, but there had been no reaction, no falling, no sudden onset of clumsiness.

She took her hair again, a smaller clump this time, holding it higher, closer to her head. Her right hand raised itself, as if to deliver a blow, then came down to join the other hand and begin its cutting, sawing and hacking at the long hair. Stephanie felt it falling around her, lank tresses brushing past her on their descent to the floor. She dipped her head and turned, twisting around, spiralling so that the hand could reach the hair, the air cool on her neck.

A boy was looking at her, his hair spiky and shorn, his face small in the mirror, the ears gawky. Stephanie smiled at this new person, who smiled back. Too friendly, she thought. She sneered and scowled. Was this Delmont? Stephanie thought she could see something of him there, something of his charm and his grace, his open agreeable countenance, his manliness. She brought the scissors back to her head.

The Doctor

She would need a doctor for the duel. That was important. A doctor had attended Delmont, would attend Delmont. The doctor must be warned, the doctor must know but not know. The only doctor she knew was Dr Sweeting. 'Such a naughty man!' her mother had exclaimed, cheeks reddening, unable to keep the excitement from her voice.

'Naughty? He's senile if you ask me.'

'Not when he was younger, dear. Anyway, it's nothing. It's just...'

Her mother did that, like a stage play, leaving sentences unfinished, waiting for the other character to pick up the cue. Stephanie played the part.

'Just what?'

They had been in the car, driving back from the doctor's. Her mother had called her bluff, insisting that if Stephanie were to miss another day's school, she had to at least go to the doctor's to find out what, if anything, was wrong with her. Stephanie was good at being ill. She could convince even herself sometimes that she really was ill, that there was something incurable inside her. It had not been difficult to persuade Dr Sweeting. Fittingly for a man in his position, he had an enthusiasm for illness, it justified everything about him, the smell, the days spent sitting in the surgery in his house.

'I asked him if he could syringe your brother's ears,' she said. Then she giggled, her eyes dreamy, only imagining the road as it rolled beneath the car.

'I don't see what's rude about that.'

'I said, 'Do you blow in ears?''

'And?'

Her mother was smiling, a stupid, tipsy smile, Stephanie thought.

'Oh, I can't tell you, dear,' she said, awakening. 'Not till you're older.'

Stephanie was older, although her mother had not realised. The doctor was older too, his frayed clothing and messy surgery betraying an increasingly befuddled mind.

It was difficult for Stephanie to know her mother's age. Muriel – although she was always Mother to Stephanie – had always prided herself on keeping her age a secret, as if she was in possession of some sacred formula that must be shielded from the rest. The coquettishness she displayed when asked about her age had the effect of making her seem both old and young, the puckered lips and fluttering eyelashes calling to mind a silent movie star, shielding herself from the advances of a young buck or some ageing lothario.

'Do you think he'd come out?'

'Who dear?' Her mother was still imagining the young doctor of her dreams.

'Doctor Sweeting. Do you think he'd come out?'

'What do you mean come out? Come out where?'

'Come out to see me. If I really needed him to.'

'Well he does home visits, dear. Don't you remember he came to see your brother when he was so ill?'

Yes, she remembered. Of course she remembered. Her

mother knew that she would remember. It had been not long after their father had gone, the grief and the emptiness filled by Matthew and his ailment. The doctor had come after her mother had called him on the telephone, whispering in the hallway, cupping her hand over the receiver.

'Oh, Doctor, that would be so good of you. I really don't know what's wrong with him. It's as if, well, he's so weak, just lying there. He doesn't seem to have a temperature, but he won't eat. He barely talks.' This last was delivered with an air of triumph, as if the silencing of Matthew was incontrovertible proof that something was very wrong, that he had finally succumbed and could only be saved by the intervention of an external force. Stephanie had listened, sitting at the top of the stairs, not sure where she should be in the house as her mother carried on with her private melodrama, her voice rising and falling. The showiness of it all made Stephanie recoil. She wanted to hide, burrow down, bury herself in her skin and not be exposed to the shrillness. Her mother had been like this for as long as Stephanie could remember, although she doubted whether it had always been the case. Would her father have fallen in love with this woman? They had met at university, in a distant time, full of the optimism of the post-war. Her mother liked to regale Stephanie with the story of seeing this dreamy man in an air force blue bomber jacket, part of a group of friends, yet not really part of anything. She was the former head girl, the leader of her group, the determined one who would make something of herself, who would take to heart her parents' urging to better herself. He was neither in the air force nor at the university, yet was able to muster the quiet charm to be welcomed into any group he wished to join.

Her father had always seemed so calm to Stephanie's young eyes, his languid detachment the opposite of her mother's determined neediness. After he had gone, Stephanie would wonder whether that could explain his drinking, why her charming father had become the gruff presence in the house, the one to be avoided, the one who would tell the children off with needless, thoughtless force, chastising them for misdemeanours that only he could perceive. Stephanie had struggled to understand the changes in his mood and had taken to approaching him as an animal would a potential predator, shying away, removing herself from his presence. By the end he did not notice, his eyes glazed, staring into space, isolated by the alcohol, his body clock ticking off the moments until he could legitimately have a drink. She had seen him one afternoon in the kitchen, pouring vodka into a glass and hurriedly swallowing it, throwing back his head, tossing the liquid down into himself. To Stephanie, he had looked frightened, a man in flight from his life, from the realisation that he had marooned himself inside a lie that he could not sustain with a woman he could not abide.

Stephanie had shut herself away from her parents' screaming, blocking the noise out as if the rows were taking place somewhere else, not part of her life. There had been an escalation, a stripping away of veneers as the arguments evolved from whispers to hissing to shouting, doors slamming, crashes and bangs behind walls, the sound of lives shattering. As all had fallen around her, Stephanie's mother had taken refuge in her son, enveloping him, leaving Stephanie to fend for herself. They had left her, Stephanie reasoned, without honour.

The doctor had arrived shortly after the phone call had ended, bustling in through the door, taking his shoes off even though they weren't muddy; in any case, Muriel had insisted on all the carpets being covered with clear plastic mats when they had moved into the house, a touch that bestowed an air of impermanence to their presence. The doctor's voice filled the house, occupying the muffled space as if he was the host at an awkward party.

'Now where's young Matthew?' he had declared.

'It's just Matthew,' said his mother. 'We only have one Matthew now.'

'Ah, yes, of course. Matthew.' There had been a silence, a marking of the passing of time. The doctor had peered up the stairs, as if looking for a way through a clearing in the woods. 'Don't worry about me, I'll find my own way.'

Just one Matthew. Stephanie had always been at a loss to understand why there had ever been two. If she had been born a boy, would she have been named Matthew too? What sort of a man would name his son after himself? What sort of a woman would allow her son to be named after the father? Matthew went through life as if he was unaware of it, had not deigned to notice that he shared his father's name. It was rarely mentioned, as if it were a genetic trait better ignored in polite company, a stutter that went unheard. As a point of honour her father never defended it as something to be proud of. He never proclaimed that he had named his son after himself, that he had shared the gift of his name with his only son.

He had ignored it, as he did with everything else, simply kept his head down in the hope that nobody would notice. It was one of the things they argued about, Stephanie's parents, her mother screaming at her father, and him muttering smug lines of justification to himself. Why wouldn't he say what he was thinking, she would demand. Just something, just once, but he would prefer to feign indifference, or indecision, while all the time doing everything he could to manipulate events to suit his wishes, to assert himself as passively as he could. Even the naming of the children, calling the son after the father, he managed to persuade her was her idea, that he had been the unwitting recipient of a gesture of unfathomable largesse, that really it was something he would never dream of.

'Melancholia,' the doctor had pronounced on descending the stairs. He had prescribed a tonic, something so thick and disgusting that Matthew had refused to take it and Stephanie had drunk it for him. Muriel had filled the days with a frenzy of chores, believing that grief could be alleviated by housework, cleaning and dusting as if it were spring, the heat of summer burning through the windows as they polished and rubbed the glass, seeing the land beyond washing in and out of focus. They had cooked for an army, plastic containers filled with stews and shepherd's pies and Bolognese sauce placed methodically in the freezer in the garage, her father's garage, terrain only now being explored by his children. Her mother refused to enter, saying it was for them now, the 'now' redolent, a word that would forever mean after, that would signify the moment beyond the change that had come to their lives, the time that followed the event that was never mentioned.

Stephanie remembered all this as she stared out of the car window, watching the woods as they passed by, trees moving across each other on the hillside like props in a puppet theatre, the ones closer to the road hurrying past, moving faster than the beeches fringing the woods in the distance. She felt uncomfortable, alert. Her mother had never before spoken of that time, the days after their father had left them, those hollow days, when Matthew had lain in his bed. The doctor had come out for Matthew in his time of need. He wasn't as capable now as he had been then, but his incapacity, his forgetfulness, his tendency to wander off in his thoughts and talk about a past that might, for all his listeners knew, be imaginary, made him more suitable for the role Stephanie had in mind. He would come out for her, she would make sure of that.

The Assignation

Dr Sweeting was trembling. He was trying not to, one hand holding the other wrist, but a tremor ran through him, an edge of unease taking hold of his being, cutting through the fog of uncertainty that seemed to have enveloped him. He sought refuge in the familiarity of routine: he polished his glasses, taking them off to hold them up to the light, holding the end of his tie in one hand, glasses in the other, the wooden chair turning and rocking as he leaned his thin frame into it. Around him were arranged the accoutrements of his position: medical books, their green and red spines staring down at him, prescription pads and notebooks, the stethoscope, the medical textbook open on the desk as if poised to offer a diagnosis. Increasingly, he found, it was unclear what role these items played.

He had been at home when Stephanie had rung the bell, sitting in the surgery off the hallway, the room that contained his life. He had pressed the buzzer to admit her, the normal practice for out-of-hours patients.

'How are we today?' he had enquired, or some similar formulation, perhaps 'And what can I do for you?' or 'What seems to be the matter?'

'I don't have a condition, Doctor,' she replied.

Dr Sweeting was a long, thin man with a long, thin face. In a few years he would become stooped. Not long after that, gaunt would be the word people would use to describe him. His height was gradually being battered down by the door frames in his house, like a nail being hammered into a floorboard.

He lived in a modest property in a quiet street not quite in and not quite out of the town. The house came with the position of GP to the area, rather like the nearby vicarage, and although his predecessor was hunched and round-shouldered, Sweeting, showing an exemplary lack of diagnostic skill, had not associated the man's posture with his surroundings, assuming instead that he had always borne the curvature of the spine that so defined him. Sweeting had hit his head just the once as he had looked around the property. By the time of his first surgery in the house, the day after he moved in, he was sporting a plaster across the upper part of his forehead, as if he were testing a treatment for his new clients. None of them found it necessary to remark upon the appendage, given the frequency with which his predecessor sported cuts and plasters on his head.

Each morning he was aware of how the years had passed as he eased into his chair at the beginning of surgery and listened to the muffled voices and coughs in the waiting room, awaiting the knock and the procession of ailments, tiresome in their familiarity, their bearers for some reason surprised by their sudden onset, as if these things had never happened before, were not preordained. He had come to understand that his fascination with medicine had not been some Hippocratic undertaking but more of an exercise in the expression of power. Why else had he endured so many days of relentless coughs and tickles, dispatched so many pills and salves? That surge, the feeling of dominance, had sustained him through 40 years. He knew the symptoms now, of course. He had learned that on the job. The creak of the knees, the throbbing along his forearm as he climbed the stairs, the blankness that entered his mind when he sat down at his desk turning to anger at his inability to remember what he had intended to do.

Having explained the purpose of her visit, Stephanie sat silently before him, cold eyes looking expectantly at him. She watched as he rehearsed his repertoire of movements, a series of attitudes struck in the way a fencer might assume the successive positions of his craft: *Première position pour tirer l'epée, Position pour la garde en quatre, Première position du salut.* He replaced his glasses on his nose and turned to face her.

'I'm not sure we do that any more, Stephanie. There was a time of course when doctors would be routinely called to attend, indeed they were part of the ritual.'

'I know,' she said, interrupting him. 'I've read about it.'

Her hands were pulling at the edge of her coat, bony fingers picking at the frayed hem.

'You have to be there,' she said, her voice small, 'there has to be a doctor. Look.' Her hands ceased their picking and found a purpose, searching through the coat, foraging like an animal before they found a pocket and emerged bearing some pieces of paper. She offered the pieces to the doctor.

He took the papers, feeling the fragility of age between his fingers as he unfolded them. The symbols made no sense. He could see numbers and some crossings out but the words themselves were invisible to him.

'Why don't you read it to me?' he asked her, pushing it back into her hands.

She looked at him, like a gambler racking up scores, and took back the paper.

'A melancholy event,' she began. Dr Sweeting sat forward, his attention fixed on the girl before him. She seemed to disappear into the story, her breathing changing, becoming shorter as the story reached its inevitable conclusion. Sweeting, too, felt his pulse quicken.

'The doctor, on probing the wound in his chest, at once declared its dangerous character. It was found that a ball had entered his left side, and passed through his body, coming out at the chest; and had also wounded his left arm.'

The doctor was staring past her, his pale blue eyes seeing something far away. He brought his eyes down to her:

'How does it end, this story?'

'It is understood that Heazle set out on foot, and walked up the towing path of the canal on his way to London. It was said that he died in the West Indies soon after his escape. Sargeaunt returned to the Grange, sent for his clothes chest, took off his regimentals, put on plain clothes; and, at nightfall, departed on horseback, and so escaped.'

Dr Sweeting blinked several times, his eyes watering.

'Don't worry, doctor,' she said brightly. 'The bullet didn't kill him.' She turned back to the papers.

'Delmont lingered until the following Tuesday, and then expired. It was said that the nurse had given him a lotion which was intended for bathing the wounds, – instead of the draught which he ought to have taken; and that the remedies administered to get rid of it, or to neutralize its effects, produced a new internal haemorrhage, which probably accelerated his death a few hours.'

Sweeting remembered tales of physicians being present at duels, as essential a part of the performance as seconds, each duellist having their own doctor to attend to their wounds. Sometimes the doctors would turn their backs on the duellists, so they could say that they had not witnessed the act but had merely attended to the wounded. There were stories, too, of doctors joining in the fighting, of becoming so impassioned that they had set to each other, one physician slashing wildly at the other.

He gathered himself. It was madness, he knew that. Nevertheless, there was something about it that appealed to him, to his reckless side, the side that he had once known so well but had become so eroded that it was unrecognisable, forgotten.

'I was once present at a duel, you know.'

The girl started, eyes wide. Before she could say anything, he carried on. 'It was in a wood, very early in the morning. And,' he paused, struggling to remember, 'there were two men, very dashing, both in frock coats and top hats.'

He frowned.

'I think it may have been a picture. How funny, I was sure I was in it.'

He took his glasses off and began to clean them with the bottom of his tie.

'Now, why do you need a doctor, Stephanie? It's not real. You can just pretend, mark out the paces, turn and fall. That would be fun, to do it in the spot where there had once been a duel. I can't see why you need a doctor, though. It's not as if anyone is going to get hurt.'

Stephanie stared back at him, holding the older man's eye.

'It has to be real, Doctor Sweeting,' she said, 'otherwise, what's the point, where is the honour? We might as well just play make believe in the front garden. There must be a doctor and a second and the two duellists, and there has…' She stopped, her face flushing bright red.

After she had gone, he sat in his chair, in his study, looking around him. The surgery was a mess, he could see that. It did not interest him, had become a chore, something to attend to with the minimum of involvement. He looked down at his hands, stretching out the fingers, holding them taut. They were old, an old man's hands, beyond middle age. When had that happened? He had prided himself on his hands, had been fastidious about their appearance, manicuring and scrubbing, aware of his patients' eyes following them as he manipulated the tools of his business, as he pressed a sternum with two fingers, aware of the respect that his hands bestowed upon him.

The girl had intrigued him. He had not recognised her at first, assuming that the figure with the cropped hair was a boy. Even when she had spoken, he had not registered that this was Stephanie, Matthew's daughter, the member of the family he had sensed flitting through the shadows of their house, barely registering. The hair gave her an air of menace, an attitude. He had not noticed her ears before. Unprotected, they bore an indignant redness, as if affronted at the exposure, making the girl appear both angry and impatient. Indeed, she did not, he concluded, look like a girl at all, although he struggled to say that she looked like a boy either. Nevertheless, shorn of her hair, she had an intensity that he found unnerving. The sensation reminded him of the early flushes of infatuation in his youth, the lurch through the stomach bringing with it the knowledge that he was about to embark on something foolhardy, something that could not be fulfilled, that could never properly be part of him but that regardless had to be pursued.

He tried to remember if he had agreed to her outlandish proposal. Nothing bad could come of it, he was sure of that. A childish game, with him, an adult, as moderator. Perhaps she thought he would turn his back at the crucial moment, just in case.

He must get his bag ready. He remembered reading an account of a duel in which each physician was equipped with 'the necessary apparatus for tying up wounds or arteries, and extracting balls'.

She had left him with a strange question. 'Do you know where I can get a gun?' she had asked. He had wanted to suggest using swords, or fencing epées, but had thought better of it. He was about to tell her about the German duelling schools, how students wore their scars like a badge of honour, how a nick to the cheek was an essential part of becoming a gentleman. Instead he had ignored her query, feigning the deafness that was increasingly becoming part of him, and she had departed.

The Copse

She hid in the trees, willing herself to be as the thin, straight birch. Through their screen she could see the field and the hedge beyond, the light of the afternoon feeling its way up the slope. She listened to the silence, to the birds moving among the foliage high above her. The two recruiting officers were in their uniforms, jackets unbuttoned, black hats on the ground, a pouch open next to them. They were chatting, friends stretched out on the grass, propped up on one elbow, passing the time, waiting. She wondered if, even then, they knew what it was they were waiting for.

Delmont resolved never to give an apology. The reluctance to apologise was no doubt founded on the idea that doing so was unbecoming a soldier.

They had chosen pistols, not sabres, Delmont and Heazle. There was a sureness about pistols. The flailing of swords, the uncertainty of the parry and the thrust, could be avoided. Instead there would be the security of the ritual of the pistol, of one shot following the next in an orderly, pre-arranged manner. The rules of the duel were stern and precise. Steps should be taken, one combatant should follow the other in shooting. If a pistol jammed or did not fire, the test should be paused, adjustments made. Nothing would be left to chance. If the distance were too great, it should be reduced. Forty feet, twenty feet, six feet, arm extended, combatants to stand sideways on. Was this what they spoke of? Perhaps they did not know, or thought that they would somehow be immune to the introduction of lead propelled from the barrel of a pistol into the body, that their flesh would resist the arrival of base metal. They wore bright colours, like robins strutting through winter's bleak waste, their long boots polished to a sheen, the sun glinting from the buckles around their waists. They passed a thin clay pipe between them, the smoke drifting lazily up towards the sky, its trail undisturbed by any breeze until, clear of the tops of the trees, it spun around on itself and danced away into the light. She wanted to shout to them, opening her mouth to call, but nothing would come.

Where the two men were sitting was sheltered, hidden from view on one side by the copse where Stephanie had stood and on the other by a tall hedge. She picked her way through the woods, following the line of the trees edging the field. She need not have worried. They could not see her. At times, as she stepped through the brambles, they would be gone, the field empty. Then they were there again, laughing and pushing each other, chewing on cob nuts, passing the pipe back and forth.

Stephanie came to the hedge, thick with the green of summer. She reached through to part the leaves and gasped as her hand was caught by a blackthorn, its barb drawing blood, a small crimson bubble oozing from the tip of her finger. In moments the bubble had turned into a drip, and the drip into a flow. She couldn't understand how so much blood and so much pain could come from one tiny thorn. Dazed, she stood watching the blood drip to the ground. She sat on the warm earth holding her finger at the base, pressing with her thumb, squeezing hard, the colour of her skin changing from white to pink to red, all the time the blood leaving her body. She wanted to lie down, to rest herself in the ground, to let her body heal for a moment in the earth.

The wind had risen, as if a storm was stirring, whistling through the trees, their leaves jerking a crazed jig to disturb the stillness of the wood. Above the noise of the wind, Stephanie could hear the patter of rain, its drops borne on the breeze. The sun was still shining, and she could see the silver husks of the raindrops as they sped through the sky, pushed along by the wind until they too fell, released, to join with the land.

The men had gone again, their presence dispersed by the sudden summer storm. She strode out through the newly damp grass to where they had been. There were shapes set in the long grass of summer, the imprints of two figures.

She had seen a horse die once. She knew how it would happen, the mare falling to her knees, her knobbly joints ungainly, her bulk teetering before settling, raising herself on her side then rolling back, and finally, at the end, two brief exhalations then nothing, the eyes dead, unseeing. A callous flick at the eyeball confirmed that there was no life left, that the carcass was empty. Afterwards, when it had been winched on to a trailer and taken, she had lain in the impression in the ground, feeling the shape where the horse had lain, spreading herself out in what little the horse had left behind.

She lay herself down where the two men had been, feeling their bodies in the ground. Is that how it would be for her, for Delmont? Would she, like the horse, fall and struggle to raise herself? She pursed her lips and blew out, once, then twice, feeling the breath course across her lips, her dead breath. Would she fall? Had she already fallen? Dare she fall any further?

The Search

The shop smelled of age, a blend of camphor and stale sweat; dust and decay hung in the air. It was one of several in the town, each bearing the name of a well-known charity, logo plastered above the doorway in bold cheerful colours. Stephanie pushed her hands through the tightly packed racks of clothing, old lives, forgotten bodies pushing back against her, resisting the intrusion. She turned her head away, reaching for breathable air, before turning back to the ranks of old coats.

'You won't find what you're looking for. Not here.' Stephanie had forgotten about the man in the stained grey sweatshirt sitting on the stool next to the counter. For such a large man, his voice was unusually thin, a sing-song nasal whine. He hadn't moved, as if the slightest change in position would cause his bulk to overbalance and he would be thrown from his perch. He was staring balefully at Stephanie, and she wondered for a moment if he had spoken. She looked around the shop, seeing past the lampshades and the metal shelving, watching herself in the display of mirrors as she wheeled around in the small space. There was nobody else in the shop, and she was sure that it hadn't been her stray thoughts finding voice.

Stephanie nodded at him and turned back to the racks of clothing, letting her fingers brush along the procession of limp sleeves, imagining she was the queen shaking hands at some ghastly reception. There seemed to be clothes for every occasion, racks and rails with hangers packed so tightly together that it was impossible to tell what was what.

'If it's uniforms you want, you'd be better off at the costume shop.' The 'you' was pronounced 'yow', like a drawled exclamation. Stephanie stared at the man. He held her gaze, looking back at her. She started to say something but thought better of it, instead biting her lip, eyes fixed on the man, waiting. She wondered how he knew what she was looking for. She was sure she hadn't told him when she had come in the shop. In fact, she was certain they hadn't even exchanged a 'Good afternoon' or any other greeting.

'They've got everything there. All sorts. Cossacks, Cromwellians, cowboys.' He began to laugh, his body vibrating, starting at his belly, while his face was turning red. 'If it's older you're looking for they've got the lot: Hanoverian, Portuguese, French, Danish, Prussian.'

'I want uniforms,' she confirmed. She decided not to look at the man while she was speaking. She didn't like looking at him. It wasn't nice. She used her haughty voice, 'One for the 82nd regiment and one the 3rd, the Old Buffs.' She listened to her words, saw them hang in the air. There was a sound, the squeak of wood being rubbed against wood. Stephanie watched the man's reflection in the window lumbering towards her, shifting his bulk with surprising agility through the teetering piles of goods stacked in the shop.

'If it's the British army it has to be red,' he said, 'to strike terror into the enemy. Funny thing is, they said the red tunic made the British look like dressed-up monkeys.'

He came to a stop next to her, body heaving, his chest

emitting a wheezing sound. 'We don't get old things like that here,' he said, his voice distorting the vowels so that Stephanie had to watch his mouth to understand what he was saying. 'Not really old. Mostly it's just bric-a-brac, old suits, anoraks. We get a lot of coats.' He nodded at the rail in front of Stephanie, the one she had been looking through. 'Sometimes you see the same clothes come in and out, like they're on a conveyor belt, people bringing them in, then buying them again, then bringing them back.'

The man paused, looking expectantly at Stephanie.

'I see,' she said, brightly.

'Furniture,' he said, 'now, furniture is different. Not at all the same as clothing. Furniture, people will bring it in and that's it, they never want to see it again, they want shot of it. They've moved on, they don't want it in their lives any more, they've outgrown it. Not clothing. Clothes, they keep coming back. I think,' he edged a little closer to Stephanie, who responded by moving a corresponding distance away, 'it's the smell.' He nodded at her, as if he had included her in some vital charity shop truth.

'Some people just bring everything they've got. Especially at the end. Making plans, a lot of them, for eventualities, clearing things up, making sure everything is in order.' He carried on, his whining voice ascending and descending. Stephanie started to feel sick, not just queasy, but physically sick. She could taste the bile rising at the back of her throat. She looked around, but she was hemmed in by the man's bulk on one side and a nest of tables bearing an assortment of mismatched crockery on the other.

'I thought you might be one of them at first.' Stephanie tried to listen to what he was saying, but could still feel the bile at the back of her throat. 'Putting your affairs in order, even if you was very young. You had that air about you, but you don't seem to be bringing anything, not so far as I can see.'

The man let his gaze travel down Stephanie's body, turned and swayed back to the seat behind the counter, his mission complete.

'You should go to Mrs Ripley's if it's authentic you want, if you want it to look lifelike. She'll have what you need.' The man was sitting again, staring vacantly ahead. Stephanie opened her mouth to speak but had nothing to say. The sign on the shop door said open, which meant that to the outside it said closed. She picked her way through the bookcases and displays of lives past, reached for the doorknob and twisted, pushing at it. It was dark outside now, the blackness casting the lights of the shop back in on themselves, cars streaking up the street, white lights spilling on to the pavement. She saw the man move again, watched his reflection distort in the glass of the door, smudging as it slid across the window. He stopped behind her, his arm reaching out, forwards.

'It's past closing time,' he said. 'You need to turn the lock.' She could feel his breath on her hair. It smelled of moth balls. 'And then pull.'

He pulled the door back in towards Stephanie, causing her to take a step back. She felt the rolls of fat around his waist shift as she pressed against him, squeezing back into his body to let the door open.

'Go on,' he said. 'You should be alright now.'

The Asylum

'You're mad. Bonkers. You should be in here, except you are in here.' Derek was warming to his theme. 'Tell you what, when we all go home, we'll take your key off of you and you can stay here with the rest of them.' He sat back and looked around the room, laughing. 'Here, Angela. What do you think? Leave Stephanie in here. She'd fit right in, don't you reckon?'

'Leave it, Derek, will you. I'm trying to read.' Angela leaned forward to flick her cigarette ash into a plastic cup. 'You ignore him, love,' she said to Stephanie without raising her eyes from the pictures in front of her. 'That's what I do.'

Stephanie looked from Derek to Angela. It was only her fifth weekend as a cleaner but already she felt institutionalised. Working at the hospital was something of a rite of passage for teenagers in the town. Most of the people Stephanie knew had worked there or had brothers or sisters who had worked there, but none of them lasted very long. Some said it was the smells, the disinfectant, the shit, the urine, the food. Some couldn't stand the monotony of it, shining the same floors, pushing the same buffing machine along the same green corridors, bumping into the same skirting boards hour after hour. For others it was the patients, locked in, locked up, lifers.

Diagnosed and medicated, few of them knew where they were, and the ones who did, the ones who talked about it all the time, who analysed their situation, their predicament, were fantasists. They were the dangerous ones.

Stephanie's brother had got her the job, bringing her in as his replacement so that he could spend more time with his books. He'd taken her in one Sunday at 7am to meet the two supervisors, Mr Kirkbride and Mrs Macleish, the Scottish mafia, as the other domestics called them. Mr Kirkbride and Mrs Macleish occupied a room on the top floor of the Victorian hospital. Nestled under the eaves, with a view through a dormer window of the grounds – and any potential escapees, domestics or patients – they appeared to do little other than to smoke cigarettes and drink tea (Mrs Macleish) and instant coffee (Mr Kirkbride, white, two sugars). The pair ran the staff rota, directing who should go where and for what purpose, which floor should be polished, which ward should be cleaned. They also hired and, frequently, fired the domestics. Once a day, shortly before 11.30, when Mr Kirkbride had finished his mid-morning coffee, they would carry out the inspection, Mr Kirkbride jangling his heavy set of keys – one for each door in the building, he liked to proclaim – as he stood in the entrance to a ward while Mrs Macleish strode in barking commands interlaced with coughing provoked by the abrupt removal of the stream of smoke upon which her breathing depended.

'You seem like a nice enough lassie,' Mrs Macleish had declared when Matthew had presented Stephanie to them, assuring them that his young sister had some experience of cleaning. 'Why don't you start on Fawcett 2, see how you get on?'

'Is there nae anything you want to ask, love?' Mr Kirkbride had offered, but Stephanie had blushed and looked at the floor, assuming this to be the correct response in what was her first proper job.

Derek and Angela were regulars, full-time domestics, lifers themselves. They'd seen a procession of teens like Stephanie come and go, trained them, shown them how to use the heavy machines, where to clean, where not to clean, taught them the tricks and dodges of the job, how to react to the inmates, and then watched them vanish, their places taken by the next young recruit.

Stephanie had been with them since that first morning, and now realised that the vision of efficient cleaning she'd been shown that day was an act that had lasted for just those first few hours. By the second weekend, clad in the grey tunic she'd been given by Mrs Macleish, Stephanie understood that although Derek did the talking, it was Angela who was responsible for the work. Derek spent most of his time in what was euphemistically referred to as the domestics' cupboard. A windowless closet set off a dead-end corridor on Fawcett 2, the cupboard had once provided storage space for brooms, buffers and mops. All that was left of its former purpose was a set of shelves bearing bottles of industrial cleaning fluid. The rest of the space had been given over to creating what its principal inhabitant liked to term Derek's Den. In the centre of the small room was a low table, its white surface stained with the ring marks of innumerable coffee mugs. Ranged around the table was a disparate collection of wooden armchairs, the plastic-clad foam cushions exhaling in sympathy every time one of their occupants was obliged to lever themselves up.

'You can't do a duel. What do you want to do a duel for? Nobody fights duels any more. You might get hurt. Like I say, you'd be better off in here. At least you'd be safe, wouldn't she, Angie?'

Angela sighed, and her chair sighed with her as she pushed herself up. She nodded at the clock on the wall.

'Eleven o'clock,' she pronounced, and turned to the door. Stephanie and Derek looked at her, then at each other, waiting to see who would make the first move.

'Better get on then,' said Derek. 'The Mafia will be round soon.'

Eleven o'clock was the signal for Derek to make one of his rare forays on to the ward. He picked up a dirty cloth from the shelf next to the sink.

'Might come in useful,' he said with a smirk, twirling the cloth in his hand. 'Come on, girl. Follow me. Let's have some fun.'

In his early thirties, Derek had worked his way up the domestic ladder, from weekend worker while still at school to the senior cleaner on the ward. He still had the swagger of youth, his energy and desire to be at the centre of things obscuring the thinning hair as much as his attempts to comb dye into it or to style the fringe in such as a way as to disguise the retreat of his hairline.

Derek was one of the few people Stephanie allowed to call her Steph. A lot of people tried, assuming that she would be happy for her name to be abbreviated for their own convenience, or for them to assume a level of familiarity or even friendship that she did not aspire to. She normally cut them short with a simple: 'It's Stephanie.' With Derek it had been different. His may have been a squalid empire, but he was the emperor. Like the prisoner in charge of cigarettes on the block, Derek had things that people needed. He had a key for every ward, every door in the building, even for Eastergate. He'd shown Stephanie the ECT suite once, never used now but still kept in a state of readiness, just in case, with its bed with straps and a weird head collar that had made Stephanie shiver. He'd also let her see the isolation cell, a square room with soiled padding up the walls and a window high up out of reach, like the window in the attic. She hadn't gone into either room, standing instead at the threshold, teetering on the edge but not crossing over to the other side. In one room there was a line of four hooks set in the ceiling.

'Bet you can't guess what they were for,' Derek had said to her, holding the door open, the still air inside sealed within the room.

Stephanie had swallowed, her mouth dry.

'Look like meat hooks, don't they,' he'd said, 'like you get in the butchers.' He'd turned to her, a smile on his face, a smirk, cruel. 'It's where they used to hang them when they got a little too frisky, hang them in their straitjackets. Wrap 'em up nice and tight and string them up there for a bit. That would calm them down.' He flicked the switch outside the door and with a clunk darkness closed over the room. He let the door swing shut. 'Must have been quite a spectacle.'

Stephanie shivered again, her feet feeling light on the floor, the same floor she had polished that morning. She would dream sometimes about these corridors, about pushing her buffing machine side to side along the miles of broad green corridor, like a sailboat tacking along a river, vaguely swishing from one side to the other, the momentum of the machine the only thing that kept her moving.

Stephanie's dreams had started after the suicide. She still didn't understand why the girl had done it. She had been a patient on Anderson 1, the teenage at-risk ward, a forbidden zone in the far corner of the hospital where the more challenging young patients were put and the doors had double locks. Stephanie had spent an entire weekend buffing the blue corridor, a featureless tract that ran around the perimeter of the main building, a ribbon of blue paint set at waist height on the wall to remind the lost or the forlorn that they were on the blue route. The girl had somehow managed to get out of the teen ward. Derek said they never found out how, or whether she already had the knife with her or if she had stolen it from one of the kitchens on the open wards.

Stephanie thought that the girl was following her. She had sensed that she was there, walking behind her, keeping just out of sight, appearing as Stephanie was turning a corner, the girl dressed in a grey smock, holding her hands together in front of her, hair tied back from her face. Even when Stephanie slowed or waited for her, the girl would appear just as she gave up and carried on pushing the giant buffer. It was not until Stephanie had completed her circuit of the corridor, at the end of the entire afternoon, that she saw the stains on the floor, pools of sticky red liquid, some smeared by footprints, some of them clear, drops of violent crimson tracing a path, the path that Stephanie had taken, the path taken by the girl.

They found her slumped against the wall on the last section of corridor, not breathing, her skin as grey as her dress, the blood drained from her, let from her on to the floors of the hospital corridor, the once-clean now-dirty floors. Stephanie found herself irritated, annoyed that all her polishing had been for nothing. She left then, putting away the machine and hanging up her domestic's coat, punching her card in the machine and walking home through the grounds, climbing over the wooden fence that bordered the hospital and following along the tracks feeling hawthorn scratching at her, drawing her blood.

Stephanie followed Derek on to the ward, the smell of urine burning into her nose. Derek made straight for the day room, a large grubby carpeted area with windows along one side faced by a semicircle of the same armchairs. A television blared out at the room from high in the corner, two presenters with orange skin chatting on a sofa in front of some potted plants. Before the screen, half a dozen elderly people gazed at the television without seeing it. By the window a woman with grey hair stood pacing with her back to the room. Her green hospital nightie came down to her thighs and she wore a pair of threadbare stockings, holes gaping to reveal white skin mapped with blue lines. Her feet shuffled back and forth on the carpet, slippers moving over the floor but failing to gain any traction, so she stood in the same spot even though she was perpetually moving. Stephanie paused to look at her. She was always there; every time Stephanie had come into the day room the woman had been in the same spot, feet working, staring out at the green parkland beyond the window. When she had asked Matthew about this, he had for once looked up from his book to tell her that it was the drugs, the medication, that made the old lady pace like that. Stephanie had tried to talk to her once, but she had been neither seen nor heard, the woman continuing her steps even when Stephanie stood right in front of her.

'Come on, you lot, rise and shine!' Derek was pacing up and down in front of the patients sitting in the semicircle of chairs like the host of a TV variety show, spinning the cloth around in front of him, watching it spiral round on itself. 'Come on! Can't just sit there all day!' He moved to the end of the semicircle to stand behind a chair containing an elderly man, his bald head nodding with sleep. Stephanie looked away. She had seen this performance before. With a deft flick of his wrist Derek sent the cloth flying out so it snapped back on itself just as it caught the top of the man's head. He awoke with a start and immediately started shouting.

'Stop! Stop, the lot of you! I'll get you, you terrors! Don't think you can get away with it this time. I'm after you!' He reached for the stick propped up against the arm of the chair and attempted to get up, but he had no strength and barely moved, the chair wheezing in defeat as he settled back. Derek flicked the cloth at him again, and once more the man started shouting.

Derek was grinning, hopping about with a look of triumph on his face. 'Therapy,' he declared. 'Can't just let them sit there all day staring into space. They need some stimulus.'

Stephanie had been warned about Derek's tendency to assume the role of therapist cleaner, and the towel flicking had become a routine occurrence. Even the nurses seemed to tolerate it, apparently concurring with Derek's analysis that what the patients needed more than anything was stimulus.

Stephanie turned to see Mr Kirkbride ambling towards them. Derek held his ground, twirling his towel in his hand like a circus master with a whip preparing to face a particularly fearsome tiger, while Mr Kirkbride jiggled his keys in his trouser pocket.

The order of things in the hospital had been clear to Stephanie as soon as she had been shown into Fawcett 2. 'We don't call it a hospital,' Angela had explained when they first sat down in Derek's Den. 'It's not as if anybody comes in here to be cured.' Stephanie had already been told by her brother not to call it a hospital, but she had thought it polite to refer to the institution by the name on the blue and white sign at the foot of the long drive, a meandering strip of tarmac that lost itself among trees and fields, gradually slipping further and further away from the consciousness of the town to which it was nominally attached, isolating its inmates in a fair imitation of a country park. 'Psychiatric hospital', it was generally agreed, was a bit of a mouthful. 'Loony bin' was a lot easier.

The loonies were at the bottom, dumped in the bin and forgotten about, their days spent wandering the grounds, treading the corridors in winter, dazed on barbiturates, tongues lolling, their noses turned varying shades of blue by the medication administered with dull efficiency by the nurses. Just above them were the accidental patients, the ones who had been sane when they entered but had become institutionalised through a combination of habit and drugs. Stephanie's brother had told her the story of the woman he had met on a ward who claimed to have been there since the Second World War. She had come over from Poland as a refugee, she had told him. Lacking anywhere to stay she had sought sleep in a bus shelter, away from the elements. A policeman had found her, taken pity on the young woman and brought her to the asylum, as it was then known, in the knowledge that at least she would have a warm bed for the night. That night had become two, the two, three, and now she was still there, thirty years later, the war long forgotten, stranded like some Japanese soldier on a desert island. Matthew seemed to find it upsetting.

'She still has an accent,' he said, 'still speaks in a sort of broken English after all these years. I asked her if she wanted to go back, but she didn't really understand what I meant. I think I would take her if I could.'

Typical Matthew, Stephanie thought, all sentiment, no sense of anything practical, living a dream. That's why he couldn't cope with working in the asylum.

Domestics were only one step above patients, at least in theory, although really it was the domestics' domain even more than the nurses'. The nurses were supposed to be superior but they were too busy, they had jobs to do, trolleys full of medicines to dispense, little rows of pills, blue, pink, red, white, round, tablets, capsules, diamond shaped, oval, neatly arranged in miniature plastic cups to be tipped into expectant mouths before being discarded. The nurses and the domestics existed in an uneasy state of mutual non-recognition, dancing around one another as if the different colours of their tunics rendered them invisible to each other. Occasionally a doctor or a consultant would breeze through, often trailing a flotilla of lesser staff, student doctors, staff nurses, matrons, but their impact would be minimal, a temporary flutter in the day-to-day functioning of the machine, the inmates briefly startled by the gust of unexpected activity before settling back into their ritual torpor.

'Stephanie's going to be joining our more permanent residents, aren't you, Stephanie?'

Mr Kirkbride looked at Derek, uncomprehending. 'I'm not sure I get you, Derek,' he said.

'We're going to have to admit her, Mr Kirkbride. Lock her up in Anderson 1 and throw away the key.' He leered at Stephanie and adopted a conspiratorial whisper: 'Stephanie's going to fight a duel.' He looked at Stephanie and at Mr Kirkbride in triumph. 'She's going to get some pistols, take six paces and' – he cocked his finger and pointed it at Mr Kirkbride – 'bang bang, you're dead.'

Derek was laughing again. Mr Kirkbride looked puzzled.

'Go on,' said Derek, 'ask her if you don't believe me.'

Mr Kirkbride turned to Stephanie, the keys in his pocket momentarily stilled.

'What's he going on about, lassie, a duel? That went out of fashion a couple of hundred years ago. Mind you, not a bad way of settling an argument.'

'It's just a story, Mr Kirkbride,' Stephanie said. 'It was two soldiers, they were friends, sort of, but they fell out about something, and they had a duel. One of them got shot. The other turned before they'd done all the paces and shot him in the side.'

'He cheated?' exclaimed Mr Kirkbride. 'Where's the honour in that?'

'He fled in disgrace, Mr Kirkbride,' said Stephanie.

'So tell me,' said Mr Kirkbride, 'what does he mean you're going to have a duel?'

'We're going to do the duel, me and my brother,' Stephanie said, her voice assuming a sing-song tone.

'Matthew? I thought he had more sense than that.'

'Oh, he has. He has a lot of sense,' said Stephanie. 'But he can be easily led.' She could see that the two men were startled by the defiance and hardness with which she spoke about her brother. 'Very easily led,' she continued. 'Susceptible, my mother says. Not that it's a bad thing. It means he is sympathetic to the suffering of others.'

The two men looked at each other.

'See!' said Derek. 'I told you she was off her rocker. A duel! Madness, that's what it is.'

Derek turned to go. 'Right,' he said, with an air of purposefulness about him. 'Work to do, Mr Kirkbride. Can't stand here chatting all day.' He strode off down the hallway and out of the ward, twirling the cloth in his hand as he walked, like an old gunslinger.

'Do you know much about duelling?' Mr Kirkbride stood facing Stephanie.

'Much?' she asked.

'Do you know what it involved? It's not a game, not something to be taken lightly. It was a serious business.'

'Well, I know some things,' she said. 'I went to the library and read about it. I found out about my duel as well.'

'There have been some very notable duels,' Mr Kirkbride said. 'And some fine duellists, and I don't mean cowboys.'

Stephanie nodded.

'It was a matter of great honour, a way for a gentleman to gain satisfaction and secure his reputation. Anyway,' he looked at his watch, 'I can tell you about it some other time, if you like. You might need some help if you're going to do it properly.

You need to be careful, mind. You don't want to get hurt.' He turned to leave, following Derek out of the ward.

Stephanie swallowed. 'Do you know,' she began, but her voice was wrong, too uncertain. Mr Kirkbride's form receded into the green of the corridor. She swallowed again. 'Do you know where I can get a gun?'

Mr Kirkbride stopped. He turned and looked back at the girl with the shorn hair and the elfin face, nodded at her, a self-conscious jerking of the head, then turned and walked away.

The Game

Stephanie liked to hula-hoop. It gave her a reason to be out of the house, to have time to think. She had spent much of the summer in the front garden with her hula-hoop, gently swaying, absorbed in the rhythm of her thoughts, the hoop looping up and down and up and down. Sometimes she would count with it, just to see. She thought it was like counting sheep for other people, except they used that to get to sleep. For Stephanie the hula-hooping was more like entering a trance. She would stand there in her jeans or her leggings and watch the cars drive past, the people walking their dogs as they made their way up the lane. The ones who hadn't seen her before would raise a hand to acknowledge the figure standing in the garden, and then withdraw, tentatively, unsure whether they were interrupting a private ritual, and bustle on, heads down, not looking. For some of her neighbours, the sight of the skinny girl with the long hair and the long legs staring into space as she gyrated her hips was a provocation too far. She could be there for hours, so long that her legs would ache when she came to and would have to make herself stop, revelling in the effort needed to make her muscles obey her will. Occasionally she could not stop, could not break the rhythm, and came to believe herself to be at the mercy of the hoop of plastic with its worn logo and fraying stickers.

The mother of Lisa, a girl in her class, had taught her to hula-hoop. Stephanie did not have friends but she had been drawn to Lisa's mother. She was glamorous. She wore sophisticated clothes. She was from a foreign country, although whether she was an Austrian countess or descended from the Russian royal family depended on which playground gossip you believed. When she came to school to collect her daughter in her bright red sports car all the other children would stare at this exotic creature in the tight trousers, sunglasses perched on top of her head. Even the teachers would stare.

Stephanie decided to make Lisa her friend, taking little gifts into school for her, an apple, a drawing, and finding her in the playground at breaktime to deliver them. The girl had been wary at first, reluctant to look Stephanie in the eye, even to acknowledge her presence or talk to her. Stephanie couldn't tell if this reserve was because Lisa was used to people wanting to be her friend so they could get close to her mother in the hope that some of her mystique would rub off on them, or whether she was frightened by the otherness of Stephanie, the girl at school who didn't know anyone, who didn't know how to be friends with other children.

One Saturday in June, in the early heat of summer before the ordeal of the holidays had started, Stephanie went to Lisa's house. She hadn't been invited, didn't know if anyone would be there, but she went anyway, taking herself off and walking across the town to the posh houses, the ones with no neighbours and wooden beams in the walls, with gravel drives and tidy gardens.

Stephanie had crossed the town in a daze, oblivious to the weekend shoppers queuing in their cars to negotiate the series of roundabouts encircling the town before waiting in line, engines running, for a space in the car park. Until she reached the high street, Stephanie had not passed another person on foot, and her presence alongside the vehicles, often overtaking them as they waited, was the cause of consternation to their occupants.

The shoppers went about their business, resuming the normal interactions of civil society as if awakened from a dream while Stephanie moved through them, hearing their cheery greetings, snatches of the weekend's gossip, exchanges about the weather, the heat, how you could not breathe, how summer had come early this year and it was already hot enough to send you out of your mind, to make you do something you might regret.

Stephanie left the babble of the marketplace behind and, crossing another roundabout, headed towards the far end of town, where the houses on the sweeping avenues were spread out to such an extent that only the foolish would contemplate walking.

The sports car was outside, slotted into a garage with no door. Stephanie let her hand run along its red shell, gleaming like a beetle. The top was down, and she stared at leather seats the colour of clotted cream, good enough to eat.

'Can I help you?'

A burly man was standing under the porch of the house, hitching up his trousers.

'I've come to see Lisa,' Stephanie said. 'To play.' The words felt strange to her, the wrong taste to them. She'd heard other children talk about going to each other's houses and she assumed this was what was said at these times.

The man stood looking at her. He was ugly, Stephanie thought. He looked like a farmer, and the vision distressed Stephanie because he did not belong in that house with Lisa's mother and the red car.

'Mitzi!' he called. He took another look at Stephanie and retreated into the house.

Stephanie waited, fingertips still resting on the sleek metal of the car. She heard a movement behind her, and Lisa's mother emerged from the garden, walking across the gravel of the drive, her sandals causing a faint scattering of the white stones. She was wearing pale blue shorts and a matching bikini top, large sunglasses covering half of her face so that all Stephanie saw was red lips.

'Do you like the car?' Her voice was deep, much deeper than Stephanie had imagined.

Stephanie stared at her. 'Is it fast?' she asked. She tried to drop her voice, to match the woman's timbre, but only succeeded in sounding like her brother when his voice had not quite broken, someone stuck in a transition from which he might never emerge.

The woman smiled. 'Oh yes, it's fast, very fast.' The two stood looking at each other, the young girl, still a girl, and the grown woman, eyeing each other, the perfection of the red sports car between them. Stephanie noticed that close up the woman's orange skin seemed tough.

'You're at school with Lisa, I expect,' she said. Stephanie did not know if it was meant as a question or a statement of fact.

'Yes,' she answered. 'I've come to play.'

The woman raised an eyebrow, the fine dark line describing a perfect arc above her eye. Behind her, the tiny leaves on a rose bush flickered in the breeze.

'Lisa's not here. She's at her riding lesson.' She paused again, studying Stephanie. 'You can come and sunbathe with me, while you wait. Come.'

She turned and walked away from Stephanie and the car and back around the hedge into the garden. Stephanie had never sunbathed. People didn't sunbathe where she lived.

Her shoes scrunched on the gravel, the stones giving a little as each step settled to the ground. She was following the woman's steps, treading in the small indentations left by her feet. The woman was lying on a sun lounger at the far edge of a terrace bordering the lawn. The grass seemed unnaturally green, as if it had been painted, each blade carefully coloured and arranged to present a perfect lawn. The woman raised herself on one elbow as Stephanie approached, shielding her eyes from the sun with a hand even though she was still wearing sunglasses, the straps from her bikini hanging loose down her arms.

She gestured at the sun lounger alongside her. 'You can lie here,' she said, and eased herself back down, her face staring up at the sun, sightless.

Stephanie did as she was told, mimicking the pose. Immediately she felt sweat trickling down the inside of her shirt, a line running from her armpits and tickling pore by pore around her side to her back. She opened her eyes. The sun flared the harsh yellow of flames, and she felt a pain behind her eyes. She closed them again, but could still see the yellow orb tinged with pink through her eyelids. She waited for the pain to subside.

'It often can take a while.' The woman's voice came to her, growling through the thick sunlight. She forced herself not to open her eyes, to keep them clamped shut, letting neither light in nor the water that had collected inside them escape. 'For the sun.' Stephanie didn't know if she had been speaking all the time or if she was only hearing occasional words. 'The eyes.' Stephanie felt the sweat running down her stomach now, the heat pushing down through the sweatshirt she always wore, turning it heavy with moisture. 'Before you lose the image. It's burned on your eye, but it will go.'

Stephanie turned her head and nodded to the woman, still without opening her eyes.

'What can you see?'

Stephanie didn't know what to say. She had her eyes closed.

'Um, nothing really,' she said.

'I quite like it, that sensation. The way the last thing you saw persists, imprinted on to your retina, even though you cannot see it any more. Even though it is no longer there. All that you can see is the memory of it.'

Stephanie opened her eyes. The sun was still there. It flashed at her again. This time she forced herself to keep her eyes open, blinking through the pain, tears falling on to her legs as she sat up. The woman lay on her sun lounger, watching Stephanie from behind her sunglasses.

'Do you do this a lot?' Stephanie asked.

'When I can,' she said.

'I've never sunbathed,' said Stephanie. 'I don't think Mother sunbathes. Father never did.'

The woman pushed her sunglasses down her nose, a habit that Stephanie had practised in the mirror with her mother's reading glasses.

'You're that girl, the one in Lisa's class...'

Stephanie waited. It hadn't occurred to her that the woman had not asked her name. 'Stephanie,' she said, tired of waiting for the woman to work it out. 'I'm Stephanie.'

'That's right,' the woman said, looking over her glasses with an even more serious expression. 'My name is Mitzi. Lisa didn't mention that you were coming to play.'

'It's a surprise,' said Stephanie.

'Well, that's very nice of you,' said the woman. 'She will not be back immediately though.'

'What does she do when she plays with her friends?' Stephanie asked.

'She likes to hula-hoop,' said the woman. 'At the moment.'

'Can you teach me to hula-hoop?'

The woman laughed. It was the first time Stephanie had heard her laugh, a deep sound, like a man's laugh.

'Sure,' she said, swinging her legs round to the ground and slotting her feet into the sandals set next to each other.

She stood up and waited for Stephanie to rise, the two of them walking around the side of the house to another lawn, this one with a climbing frame and a swing facing away from the house towards the line of trees that suggested the end of the town, although in reality they had been planted there when the house had been built as part of the town's desire to have a proper suburb. Beyond it lay more roads and more houses.

Mitzi picked up a blue hula-hoop lying in the grass, lifted it over her head and set it spinning. She stood there staring at Stephanie, barely moving as the hoop looped around her in a lazy motion, as if it too had been drained of energy by the heat.

'You might want to take off your sweatshirt,' she said, and Stephanie complied, even though she was worried about the grubby T-shirt she'd put on that morning.

'You can use that one.' Without breaking rhythm the woman pointed at another hoop lying on the grass. Stephanie picked it up and looked at it. It was just a plastic tube in a circle, like a piece of pipe. The woman stopped, and the hoop dropped to the ground. Stephanie could see the heat rising on the far side of the garden, the air swimming, smudging the line where the trees met the grass.

'You need to put it over your head,' she said, walking towards Stephanie. 'Now you must hold it with both hands and spin it around your waist.'

Stephanie pushed the hoop around her waist with both hands. It circled around her legs once, twice before falling to the ground.

'You have to move your hips, Stephanie,' Mitzi said. 'Like this.'

She came and stood behind her, close enough that Stephanie could feel her breath warm on her neck. She smelt expensive. She held Stephanie gently at the hips and started to move in small circles, taking Stephanie with her.

'That's it,' she said. 'Now you can try it with the hoop.' She moved away. Stephanie retrieved the hoop from where it lay on the ground like a discarded piece of clothing, placed her feet inside it and pulled it up her body. She spun it again, and this time moved her hips in the way Mitzi had shown her. The hoop stayed with her for three or four spins and then toppled again to the ground.

'Just remember to keep your own rhythm,' Mitzi said, standing back to watch. 'The hoop will follow you.'

Stephanie tried again. This time the hoop did stay with her, the woman silently looking on as the girl moved her hips back and forth, round and round.

The Scar

The brother was in his chair, reading in the gloom.

'What are you reading, Matthew?' she asked.

He ignored her, but she could tell that he had heard by the way his brow furrowed slightly at the disturbance. He leaned further into his book, holding it up so that it would catch the sliver of light allowed through the window. Outside Stephanie could make out shafts of bright sunlight, but they served only to deepen the shadows in the house.

She tried to tiptoe across the living room floor to sneak a look at Matthew's book, but he sensed her movement, or felt the air move, and snapped the brown covers closed.

'What are you reading, Matthew?' she asked again. He let out a theatrical sigh, the way adults do to children when they finally have to turn from what they are doing to attend to some demand, and raised his eyebrows at her expectantly.

'Yes, Stephanie,' he said, taking off his glasses. She thought he was going to clean them, like Dr Sweeting. 'What is it?'

She looked at him. Were they still children? Could you still be children if you didn't really have parents? Matthew had their mother, but she seemed to be more his companion than his parent. Who did she have? She had grown up, in the time since, she was aware of that. Matthew looked older, taller, he was filling out, his body thickening, the change from skinniness to solidity.

She used her commanding voice, the firm one.

'We're going outside.'

'Stephanie,' he said. 'I'm reading.' He attempted to turn in his chair, opening the book and positioning it before the light.

'You're not reading,' she said. 'You're staring at the same pages over and over. You'll never finish that book and even if you do you'll just start it again.'

'That's not true,' he said, irritation alive in his voice. 'You shouldn't talk about things you don't understand.' He turned back to the book, but she could see that his eyes were not focused on the page in front of him.

'We're going outside,' she declared again, and she closed the curtain next to him, shutting out what little light penetrated the glass.

'Outside!' she said, again, striding out of the living room and waiting in the doorway for Matthew to raise himself out of the chair, pulling himself up like an old man.

'What are we doing?' he asked as he joined her at the door.

'The duel, Matthew,' she said, 'we're doing the duel.'

She led him out of the garden and up the lane. Brambles grew dense along the walls, straddling them, wrapping around them as if to smother and pull them down. Blackberries were coming now, the hard green crowns of early summer turning with the impending arrival of autumn, absorbing the last of the sun, taking the moisture from the air and blooming into plump fruit, leaving a deep stain, like dried blood, on Stephanie's hand as she went to pick them. As abundant as they were, with the green of the bush disguised by the black of the berry, it was hard to get more than a handful at a time. Before, they had gone blackberrying, the four of them each bearing a bowl from the kitchen, sleeves rolled down to protect them from the thorns or the smarting sting of the nettles that laced themselves through the brambles, and they would stand looking at the monstrous bushes, realising that while from afar the fruit had appeared so abundant and that all they would have to do was stand there and the berries would fall into their hands, closer inspection showed that the ornery bush had stacked its riches at the top, out of reach, luxuriating in the sun, while close to hand was nothing but barbs, ready to rip the skin at the merest touch.

Matthew trailed behind Stephanie as they climbed away from the town, the lane gently rising until they reached a ridge, the fields sweeping away below them, the folds of the land hiding the foot of the valley. Stephanie could sense the wildlife around them falling silent as they passed, making space for the two intruders to go on their way before the life of the land resumed.

She stopped at a gate. Matthew joined her, out of breath, his cheeks red. She had been unaware of his presence almost since leaving the house, absorbed in the world around her. A wooden sign had been fixed to the metal gate a long time ago; its letters, barely legible through the grime, spelled out the words 'Forty Acres'. To one side was a stile, and a narrow path running along the edge of the field as it descended into the valley, plunging down and away out of sight. They stood on the lane, peering into another country.

'Why do you want to go down there?' Matthew asked, as if he too had emerged from a dream.

'That's where the duel was,' Stephanie said. 'They came down here, the three of them.'

She looked at Matthew, at his young face growing old. He raised his eyes to return her gaze. His eyes had changed too, she thought. They were still young eyes, still timid behind his glasses, hiding from something, or perhaps hiding something from view. She wanted to ask him what he thought about, what he was thinking about when he was reading that book, but she sensed that the time when brother and sister could ask anything of each other had passed.

He looked away, the flash of openness obscured once more, the frown returned to its place, a slight wrinkling of the brow beneath his fringe, the pinching together of his eyebrows, as if it was something he had rehearsed in the mirror, something he had seen in an adult and practised, one of the rituals of growing up.

'Come on Matthew,' Stephanie said, 'I'll show you. There's something we've got to do.'

She put a foot on the stile but Matthew didn't move.

'I don't really think I want to,' he said, the little boy resurfacing.

'You don't have a choice, Matthew,' she said. 'It's something we have to do, something we agreed to do. No harm can come of it.'

'Why are you doing this, Stephanie?' he asked. 'It won't bring him back.'

'Come on, boy!' she shouted, the bark of the parade ground voice cutting across the stillness of the day. She grabbed his arm and pulled him with her as she went over the stile and on to the path.

Matthew followed as she walked ahead, the slight figure striding down the hill, the gradient propelling her on. To their left all was dark, the woods impenetrable, slender trunks bristling alongside thicker trees, fanning out almost as soon as they had emerged from the ground, blocking the passage of anything but the most nimble of creatures. Above, pinpricks of light pierced through the dense cover, columns of dust swirling in the gloom. Below lay darkness, the matted mulch of winter concealed by the dry waste of summer's detritus, the yellowing remains of wild garlic spreading its cloying aroma through the still air. To the right of the two duellists lay the shrill brightness of the summer, grass so green it seemed to shine. The field swept away from them, falling down the slope in a series of waves before disappearing over a ridge, leaving just the distant blue of the far side of the valley.

Occasionally they stumbled, deceived by the contour of the land or the speed of their descent, unable to decipher the obstacles that lay on the path. Once, he called to her to rest, but she ignored him, her stride uninterrupted. He was sweating now, moisture collecting under his glasses, and he was forced to take them off and put them in his pocket, rendering the land even more dreamlike.

It was at one of these moments that he bumped into her. She had stopped, suddenly. They stood, stationary, on the line between the dark of the woods and the blazing light of the field. Before them, set in the field beyond, was a small copse, a circle of trees so perfect and so incongruous that it might have been planted there for someone's amusement, or perhaps as a landmark to aid navigation.

Stephanie was alert, eyes fixed on the copse, sweat on her face, chest heaving from the descent.

'What is it?' he said, struggling to catch hold of his breath.

Stephanie stared at the copse as if watching prey, her lips slightly open, waiting.

'Stephanie,' he said again, 'what are you looking for?'

She turned to him, a hardness in her eyes. 'My name is Delmont, boy,' she said, her voice calm. 'And you are Heazle.'

She moved away from him, climbing over the wooden rail of the fence that bordered the path and striking out into the heat of the field. Immediately she felt the sun on her, hitting her eyes, blinding her, the surge of colour almost causing her to fall. Matthew, too, stumbled as he stepped into the glare.

She left a trail as she walked through the grass, its long blades bending beneath her feet, sweeping at her legs. Matthew followed, their passage leaving a line in the crushed grass that wandered as if knowing no order, yet leading inexorably from where they had been to where they were going, to the duel.

When they reached the copse they stood again, looking into it, silent, with no need for words. They walked around its perimeter, the cool of the trees beckoning them in from the heat of the field. The trees stood in a circle, sentinels facing out, ignorant of what happened within. Their trunks were woven through with brambles and bracken tinged with gold, preparing to wilt in the high death of summer.

There was an entrance of sorts, a flattening of the grass, evidence of animals having passed through in their search for shelter or food. The two figures picked their way through, shoes grasped by the undergrowth, thorns tugging at their jeans until they had passed and were inside, looking out at the sentries, seeing through the trees the heat of the field, the shimmer of colour as it travelled across the land to the darkness of the woods beyond.

Within was a small meadow, the grass pale and long, clumped into hillocks. The air was different within the ring of trees, cooler, undisturbed by heat or breeze. Stephanie paced around the edge of the copse, as if measuring it.

'We're not going to do it now, are we?'

She stopped her pacing.

'No, not now,' she said, the voce deep again, masculine. 'We haven't got a second or a doctor. How could we do it now?'

Matthew sat down on the ground.

'You said there was something we had to do.'

She came towards him, her hand reaching into her jacket

pocket as if reaching for a gun. Before he could get up she was already there, kneeling next to him.

'Don't, Stephanie,' he said, his voice trembling. 'It's not funny.'

'Don't be stupid, boy. It's only a knife.'

The Library

The man at the library counter was still smiling, as if Stephanie had only stepped out for a moment, as if he had not seen her steal the poster. His smile only faltered slightly when she turned her face to him, the eyes losing their sparkle just a little, barely enough to show.

'I'd like a book about duelling,' she said. She had practised this question too, but this one had been much easier. Stephanie didn't know if it was because she had already been to the library, already knew what the man would say, which door she should go through.

The man looked at her, his eyes glazing over as he began to speak.

'Fiction: Casanova, Chekhov, Conrad, Kuprin, von Kleist, Maupassant, Pushkin, Thackeray.' He drew breath. 'Non-fiction: Goncharov, Kipling, Lermantov, Nietzsche, Schnitzler, Turgenev.' His mouth paused.

Stephanie nodded and went through the door.

The room was different this time, unrecognisable. Instead of tables, there were rows of grey metal shelves, like life-size Meccano towering over her. The room was brightly lit, strip lights running along the narrow gaps between the shelves, a space just wide enough for her to enter. A large letter was stuck at the end of each row, the categories of the books indicated on signs hung from the ceiling: Taxidermy, Theoretical Psychology, Truancy. She looked along the rows of books at the titles written sideways on the spines, gold letters flaking off red leather, green leather, the binding of the books peeling away to reveal the cardboard beneath. She ran her fingers along the edges of the books, feeling them flick against her as she walked.

She found what she was looking for along the bottom shelf, a row of a dozen books bearing different plain covers but all with the same title in gold letters: 'The Duel'. She took one from the shelf, the smallest one, a thin book with a green cover, and held it in her hand. She was unsure whether to open it, whether to look inside it, but was frightened of what she might find. She placed it back on the shelf and moved her hand to another, larger volume, this one bound in red leather, with the words 'The Duel' in gold print; the bottom loop of the capital D fallen away.

She held the book in her hand, feeling its weight, and looked around her. She didn't know where to go. She tried to retrace her steps to the door, but the letters at the end of each row seemed different, as if they had been rearranged, and the lights made everything too bright, the edges too hard. She came to the end of a row and turned, rows of shelves strobing past her as she walked. She could hear the strip lights now, buzzing as they registered her progress through the room. She reached the end of the shelving and found herself in a corner. The sign on the end of the row told he she had reached the end: 'Z'.

She began to walk up the row but it felt smaller than the rest, as if not enough room had been left for the last letter and it had somehow been squeezed in. As she moved along the row it seemed to get narrower, the edges of the books catching against her. She realised she would need to turn sideways if she wanted to get through, and turned to face the spines of the books, watching the titles move past her as she sidestepped her way along, the letters closer and closer to her face. Stephanie kept moving but it was becoming increasingly difficult to make any progress as the shelves were packed too close together for her to pass. She had almost reached the end but the space was just too small to get through. She stood there, unsure what to do. She seemed to have become wedged where she was, although she could not understand how it had happened.

She had entered the row without any problem, but it had got smaller, even though she had been able to see to the end when she had started. She tried to calm her breathing, to douse the rising panic. As she went to move again she thought she felt the shelf behind her shift, the slightest movement, and then stop. She tried again. Once more there was a movement from the shelf behind her; she was sure she felt it this time, that the entire row had inched in on her. She breathed deeply and looked at the titles a few inches from her nose: Zaspopathy: recent research, Zellweger spectrum – causes and symptoms, Zlotogora syndrome in Europe since the Second World War, Zygomycosis and how to avoid it. She began to feel quite ill.

She was unable to move. She didn't know whether to shout, but she hadn't seen anyone else and thought it would sound stupid. There was another faint movement from the shelf behind her. She was unable to turn now, unable to even move her head to see what had happened. She swallowed, took a breath and cleared her throat. The noise sounded silly, strained, absurd. She did it again.

'Hello?'

That, Stephanie realised, was absolutely the wrong voice. Far too like a little girl stuck in a cupboard. She would have to do something more assertive.

'I need to be released from the shelving,' she shouted.

She listened to the silence around her, only broken by the faint crackling coming from the lights above. She was aware that she might be mistaken for the voice of a book crying out to be freed from the constraints of the library's classification system.

'Somebody move the shelves,' she shouted, 'I'm stuck.' That sounded much better, she thought, much more like the sort of thing a normal person would shout if they found themselves sandwiched between the shelves in their local library.

She waited, expecting to hear a door open or an alarm sound, but there was nothing. The lights continued to hum and crackle, and the blood pounded in her ears.

There was a jerk from behind her and the shelving moved once more, pressing her even further into the books, her nose buried into the spine of a volume examining the effects of zinc deficiency.

'Let me out,' she screamed.

'Ooh yes, that was greatly improved, much better.'

It was a man's voice, an excitable man's voice, high pitched with the rounded vowels of a private education.

'Who's that?' Stephanie asked, her voice quiet again.

'Come on, let's give it another go, shall we?' The man sounded like someone trying to brighten up a damp weekend at a seaside holiday camp. As he finished speaking the shelves resumed their movement. Stephanie pushed back against them, using all her strength to lever her body against the mass of books pressing into her back.

'You can't push, you know,' the man shouted. 'They're on runners. You won't be able to stop them.' He sounded annoyingly cheerful.

Stephanie felt the breath being squeezed out of her. Black spots started to appear where the lights had been.

'You've got to stop,' she said, although her voice now sounded so small to her that she could barely hear it herself. 'Please stop.'

'Really?' said the voice. 'But this is such fun!'

A face appeared at the end of the row of shelves. Stephanie could just see it out of the corner of her eye, although she was unable to move her head.

The lights were spreading, getting darker, fierce black pinpricks of darkness pushing at Stephanie's eyes. She tried to keep her eyes open but they kept fluttering closed, a heaviness dragging her eyelids down, closing down her sight. Her breathing, too, had stopped, her chest sunken, refusing to rise. Her mouth continued to move, Stephanie willing her lips to make movements.

'Please stop.'

The man stared at her, peering round the end of the shelf, only his head showing. He was late middle aged, possibly in his mid-fifties. He had a big face, a not-unkind face, with bushy black eyebrows and bulbous red lips. He wore a pair of blue glasses, with large round frames. At his throat a blue cravat was knotted, pushing out from a brown jacket. On his head was a tweed cap.

'Oh,' he said, disappointment in his voice, his mouth mirroring the shape of the word. 'Oh.'

The man's head and shoulders disappeared as abruptly as they had appeared. Gradually the shelf started to move back, first half an inch then more as the weight of the books gained momentum. Stephanie felt the pressure move away from her chest and shoulders, felt her legs and hips freed, the air rushing into her lungs. The sudden removal of the shelf caused her to lose her balance, and she fell to the floor, dropping the book on duelling that had stayed in her hands, wedged in by the other books while she had been squashed.

The man reappeared, hurrying along the gap between the shelves, a concerned look on his face.

'Are you alright?' he asked. Stephanie noticed that a crimson flush, whether from exertion or excitement, had spread across his face. 'You look very pale.'

Stephanie sat on the floor, trying to breathe. Next to her, poised on the floor where she was sitting, a pair of shiny red-brown boots bearing muscular black soles stood expectantly, dark blue jeans crisply turned up at the ankle reaching down to the top of the boots.

Stephanie could hear a noise, and realised that the man was talking again.

'I do love it when young people visit the library,' he was saying. Stephanie had the sense that had there been the space he would have paced up and down as he was talking. 'I think it's fantastic. Wonderful. All these books, look at all the stuff you could learn. It's inspirational, educational.'

He looked down at the figure slumped on the floor in front of him.

'So what brings you here?' he asked. 'What line of enquiry has tempted you into this temple of learning, this house of books?'

He bent down to pick up the volume lying next to Stephanie.

'Let's see now.' He tossed the book in his hand as he straightened up, flipping it around until the spine was facing him. He held it close to his face and then stretched his arm out, leaning his body away from it. He made a small noise to himself and with his other hand reached inside his coat. After some fumbling, the hand emerged with a pair of glasses. With the same hand he reached up to take off the large round glasses he was wearing and tried to replace them with the new pair of glasses. After struggling for a moment, the two pairs of spectacles becoming confused in his hand, he looked down at Stephanie, the colour spreading up his face.

'Excuse me,' he said. 'I'm most terribly sorry but do you think you could hold my spectacles? I can't seem to get them on with these in my hand. Thank you so much. Very kind.'

He bent down, put the glasses in Stephanie's lap and straightened up again, placing the new pair of glasses on his nose.

'The Duel,' he said. 'Terrific. Duelling.'

Stephanie looked up at him, her eyes travelling up the laces on his boots, the crease on the stiff denim of his jeans, following the line of buttons on his jacket, past the cravat which was partially obscuring, she noticed, a throat whose skin was red and saggy, to the eyes looking down at her through a curious pair of reading glasses. He opened the book, leafed through the first few pages, and came to a halt.

'Ah-ha! Excellent. The Twenty-six Commandments. This is it. Here we are.'

The man took a pace back, held the book at arm's length, and in a loud voice, as if he were delivering a stormy sermon to a particularly deviant congregation, declared: 'The first offence requires the first apology, though the retort may have been more offensive than the insult.'

He brought the book back to his face, mouthing the words back to himself, and looked down at Stephanie.

'Splendid, isn't it? What do you make of that?'

Stephanie was about to reply, probably something harsh or cutting, but just as she drew in breath to speak, noting the pain in her chest as she did so, the man raised his hand and pointed at her.

'My word,' he exclaimed, 'what is that? On your face!'

Stephanie's hand reached up to touch her cheek, feeling the

line of the scar scything down from her cheekbone towards the point of her chin.

'It's a scar,' she said. 'A duelling scar. It's a mark of honour.'

The man crouched down to look more closely at her face. She could smell garlic on his breath as he leaned into her, peering over his reading glasses at the red braid running up the side of her face.

'A duelling scar?' he said. 'But that's marvellous. You fought a duel? I must say, young man, that is the most thrilling thing I have heard all day. No, for several days. The exuberance of youth. There's nothing to beat it, you know. Absolutely nothing. You have to hold on to it, cherish it while you still have it.'

'I'm a girl,' Stephanie said, her voice strident, possibly a little too strident, she thought, but it needed saying.

The man stared at her, incredulous.

'So many surprises in one morning,' he said. 'Yes, indeed, of course, you are a girl, absolutely.' He turned his attention back to her scar. 'So tell me about that. How did you get it? Was it combat, a proper duel – I wouldn't imagine you were fighting over a lady – so what was it? Was honour preserved? Come on. Do tell.'

Stephanie looked at him, feeling herself gaining control. She waited. Just as he opened his mouth to draw in breath, she spoke.

'Why did you do that?' she said.

'What?' The man sounded confused. 'Do what?'

'That,' Stephanie answered, 'with the shelves. Why did you try to squash me?'

'Squash you?' he repeated. 'Oh no, I didn't try to squash you. That was just some fun. I do think it's first rate that a young person like you would go to the library. I thought it was so great to see a youngster in here that we should have some fun, play a game. Children like playing games, don't they? And I've always wanted to turn those big wheels on the end of the shelves, just to see if I could, to see what would happen.'

Stephanie didn't know if he was joking or trying to fool her. He looked sincere, but he also reminded her of a clown she had once seen at the circus.

'It was fun though, wasn't it?' he asked. 'And wasn't it tremendous that I did, because otherwise we wouldn't be here. You would have simply got your book, taken it to the desk and made your way home and I'd still be standing here not knowing quite what to do and not knowing anything at all about a girl dressed as a boy who has a duelling scar, a scar of honour on her cheek.'

Stephanie reached up to touch the scar, tracing the very tip of her finger along its length. It felt much longer than it was, she thought, as if it was long enough to stretch the entire length of her face.

'My brother did it,' she said, sounding small and hurt. 'With a knife.'

'How extraordinary,' said the man. 'Were you fighting? It must have been quite an argument. Was it a question of honour?'

'I made him do it,' Stephanie said. 'We were in the copse where the duel happened, and I made him scar me. I needed a scar. I wanted to give him one as well but he wouldn't let me. He ran away, said he'd tell Mother. He didn't though. He's not that stupid.'

The man was gaping at Stephanie, his mouth open. He swallowed, his Adam's apple working its way up and then back down his neck.

'Right,' he declared, standing up and pulling his coat straight. 'I think we need to go and get a cup of tea and you can tell me all about it. This is remarkable, the most exciting thing to have happened for a very long time.'

Stephanie looked up at the man. Her parents had often warned her about talking to strangers, and probably, although she couldn't quite remember, about accepting offers of tea from strange men. She was sure, though, that they hadn't actually specified men in libraries, particularly men who had tried to crush her between the shelves.

'You can tell me all about your escapades with swords and sabres and scars and duelling. How wonderfully entertaining! If it were pistols I'd be your man, pistols are my thing, but swords... Golly.'

Stephanie felt her face flushing red. She tried to keep her voice steady.

'Oh no,' she said, 'we won't be using swords for the actual duel. It has to be pistols.'

The man swallowed again. 'Well, come on,' he said. 'Chop-chop! On your feet.' He paused. 'What's wrong, don't you like tea? Of course you do. Everyone likes tea.'

The Second

On his arrival, they acquainted him with what had occurred, and asked him to accompany them to the field, declaring that, if he refused, they would go there alone. Upon this, and after an ineffectual attempt to reconcile them, Sargeaunt, unwisely and unfortunately, acquiesced.

He said his name was Garrick, and that he had been a teacher. His name meant 'Spear King', he told her. Stephanie was not sure if she believed him. They had gone to a café in the high street, rows of tattered yellow vinyl seats deserted in the mid-afternoon. A waitress in a tired overall stood at the counter looking at a tabloid newspaper. She had brought them tea, almost hot, not fresh, slopping down two white cups and saucers before resuming her position next to the till.

Garrick sipped his tea and smacked his lips together.

'Tell me how you got the scar again,' he said. His voice had gone quiet.

The woman at the till was staring at them, the open newspaper forgotten before her. She gave a start as a fly ventured too close to the blue electric element mounted on the wall behind her, sparking a crackle followed by a fizz and a wisp of smoke.

'In this book I got, it said that in Germany a hundred years ago they had societies at the universities, duelling societies, and if you didn't have a scar you weren't anybody. So the students would line up and slash away at each other hoping to get wounded. Nobody ever died but they said if you didn't have a scar you wouldn't be able to get a good job. It also said that if you wanted to marry well you needed a good scar to impress your fiancée.'

Stephanie imagined herself as a young man, Teutonic, proud, arrogant perhaps, wearing a cap and goggles to protect her eyes, practising her swordplay with one of the long sabres she had seen in a picture of a German student duel. She had seen one student wearing a nose guard and chain mail around his throat, with only his cheeks offered to his adversary.

'They said the Kaiser even had a scar from a duel. Once they were cut, they used to rub vinegar or red wine into the wound to make it stand out.'

'Mensur,' Garrick said.

'What?'

'Mensur, the societies are called Mensur. It still goes on although they are more secretive about their activities than they used to be.'

'Do they still have scars?'

'Yes,' Garrick said. 'They do still have scars. Now let me ask you a question: why are you interested in duelling?'

Stephanie told him about the box and the piece of paper with the account of the duel, and how she needed to re-enact it. She didn't tell him about her father, about how the duel would show her mother and her brother that she was worth as much as them, that she would regain some honour.

Spittle settled on his upper lip, and Stephanie watched it as she spoke, aware that he was absorbed in the story she was telling. It was then that she decided that this man who had tried to crush her in the library, wore strange clothing and took young girls to tea should be the second.

He sat silently, gazing at her through the thick glass of his spectacles. Stephanie sensed that he was still waiting for an answer to his question.

'The unusual thing about this duel,' she continued, trying to sound like a teacher might sound when talking to a colleague, although she thought that she probably sounded more like a television detective, 'is that it had only one second. Nobody really knows why, but as Heazle and Delmont were friends they probably wanted to keep their argument private, and felt it would be safer to only trust one person to help with the arrangements.'

She watched Garrick listening to her, sitting forward in his seat. He had taken his cap off when they had come into the café to reveal what had once been a bushy head of hair but was now thinning, the inadequacy of the hair accentuated by the gel that had been combed into it. The bubble of spit was still on his lip.

She decided to tell him. She would say it cheerfully, as if it were a matter for celebration, as if it had just come to her, a revelation.

'I know!' she exclaimed, her voice rising like a girl's. 'You shall be the second!'

His eyes, which she noticed were a very pale shade of blue laced with red, were staring at her but seemed not to be seeing her, as if they were focused on something very far away and not on the object in front of them. It occurred to Stephanie that she might have inadvertently hypnotised Garrick. She had spent some time a year before trying to hypnotise Matthew, sometimes with his acquiescence and at others when he was unaware, his face buried in his book. Watches and pendulums and bright lights had not worked so she had resorted to concentrating very hard and staring at the back of his head across the living room. That hadn't worked either and she had just developed a series of headaches that stayed with her for a week.

'Garrick!' she said. She wanted to shout at him to wake up but didn't think it would be appropriate. His eyes moved to her, focusing, drifting down to the scar on her face. 'You shall be Sargeaunt! You shall be the second.'

She said it quietly this time, and he nodded, as if the words had taken several seconds to cross from her mouth to his ears over the blue Formica of the café table.

'Second?' he said. 'Gosh, yes, well, do you know, yes.' Stephanie thought he might be playing for time. Either that or he was genuinely confused.

'That would be absolutely splendid. What an excellent idea.' He clapped his hands, as if to rouse himself from the hypnosis, his composure regained. He looked around the café. The waitress raised her head, ready to take offence, trying to work out whether the clap of hands had been aimed at her. 'When do we start?'

Stephanie waited.

'Start?' she said. 'We've already started.'

He watched her hand come up to the scar on her face again.

'Golly,' Garrick said. 'Do I need to get a scar as well?'

'No, Garrick,' she said. 'The second doesn't need a scar. The second just has to bring the pistols and to load them for the duellists. You said guns were your thing.'

The Pistols

Mitzi was tired. She looked through the French windows at the patio, the loungers stranded on the paving stones, stripped of their cushions, their metal frames like skeletons. One had been blown over by the wind, its feet sticking into the air, stricken. A hot wind had been blowing for days, sucking the air out of the barren countryside. Mitzi had retreated indoors, preferring to endure the chill of the air conditioning rather than suffer the claustrophobic heat of the outdoors pressing in on her. She leaned against the glass, feeling it warm against her face. She had chosen her clothes more carefully than normal that morning, putting on a Chanel all-in-one, white with gold buttons, and had painted her nails white, marvelling at the contrast with her tanned skin. Now, listening to the whistling noise the wind made as it forced its way through the window frame, she felt tired again.

She caught her reflection in the glass, the white and gold of her ensemble bright against the washed-out browns and yellows of the world beyond. On the other side of the window was the girl from school, the strange one with the cropped hair, standing on the patio with her hand raised, staring at her.

Mitzi moved back with a start, stumbling as her leg met

the arm of a chair. The girl walked towards the window and knocked on it with her fingers, her nails tapping against the glass. Behind her, a solitary magpie stood on the lawn, its beak noiselessly opening and closing.

Stephanie tapped on the glass again. One for sorrow, Mitzi thought to herself. She smiled, white teeth showing, nodded to the girl, and gestured to the window, a movement that was redundant because the girl was already there.

She pulled the latch down and heaved on the frame, feeling its weight gather momentum as it slid to the side. The girl did not move.

'Hello, Mrs Plommer,' she said. Her voice sounded grown up, Mitzi thought, confident. 'I'm sorry to bother you, but I wondered if Lisa was home? We never did manage to play.'

'That's alright, I was just...' Mitzi's voice trailed off. She hadn't been sure what she was going to say, and now she felt unsettled by this girl. 'It's...'

'Stephanie,' the girl said.

'That's right, Stephanie. You came at the beginning of the summer.'

Stephanie nodded, waiting until Mitzi noticed. She almost cried out when she saw it.

'My God!' she said.

Stephanie touched the side of her face. 'It's a scar,' she said.

'Yes.' Mitzi reached out to touch it, two fingers alighting on the tip of the scar, at the point of Stephanie's cheekbone. The girl flinched, but held her head steady as the older woman ran her fingers down the red gash, tracing the trajectory of the cut.

'Come in, please,' she said, arranging her features into a smile. 'Lisa's not here. She went to the swimming pool with some friends from school, but you can wait if you'd like, she won't be long.'

Stephanie stepped over the rail that held the window. Mitzi

leaned against the handle and it slid back into place, sealing shut with a clunk.

Stephanie looked around the room. A pair of matching white leather sofas faced each other, a low square glass table between them. At one end of the room was a brick fireplace with an angular black metal and glass stove set inside it.

Stephanie's trainers had left a trail leading from the plate glass of the window to the cold steel of the fireplace, small footprints marking her passage across the wooden floor and over a deep white rug, thick like a bleached meadow.

'There aren't many things,' she said.

Mitzi looked around her, at the clean lines of the furniture, at the polished surfaces, appreciating the control the room exhibited.

'No,' she said, 'I don't like things.' She was feeling more like herself now, invigorated by the unexpected presence of this strange child.

'It's a scar of honour,' Stephanie said, 'a duelling scar.'

'You have been in a duel?'

'No,' Stephanie said. 'My brother did it, in preparation for a duel. It is part of the process you go through to toughen the mind, sharpen the senses.'

It was as if she were reciting a code, her voice dispassionate. There was a tension in the silence that followed, the moment suspended. Neither spoke. Away from the window, in the centre of the room, there was no sound, no noise penetrated from outside, no birdsong, not the cackle of the magpie nor the sigh of the wind. Outside, the tiny leaves of rose bushes ballooned silently across the lawn, flustered into activity by the rising breeze.

'There's something I want to show you,' Mitzi announced, and walked out of the room. Stephanie followed her across the hallway with its open staircase and pale wooden floor and into the room opposite. This room was smaller, lined with books, shelves reaching from the floor up to the ceiling along one wall. Blinds were drawn across the windows, wooden slats allowing only a muted light to filter into the room.

'My husband picked them up at an antique shop, ages ago,' she said. 'It's not really his sort of thing. I think he just liked the look of them. Geoffrey is not normally one for impulse.'

She smiled and turned to the end of the room. Stephanie followed her gaze. High on the wall in the far corner hung two long pistols, facing each other, as if primed. Each pistol had a central part made of wood, and a handle encased in black metal, gracefully curved like the neck of a swan. A thick ring of engraved metal looped around the trigger, and above it extended a long hexagonal barrel.

'Do they work?' she asked.

Mitzi looked at her, elements of a smile forming on her face.

'I don't know,' she said. 'They're supposed to work but I'm not sure when they were last fired. I suppose it could be more than a hundred years ago. I don't know if they have ever been fired in anger.'

Mitzi watched as the young girl stared intently at the guns high on the wall. Her face was flushed and she seemed to sway slightly.

'Can I have them?'

Mitzi smiled. 'Well now,' she said, 'for that you should really ask Geoffrey.' The day, which had promised its routine dose of perfectly manicured boredom, had become something much more interesting. She laughed, although it emerged as more of a growl than a laugh, and looked at this curious girl, standing there, her scruffy clothes so out of place in Mitzi's world. There was something appealing about her desperation, Mitzi thought, about the drama of the scar across her face.

Mitzi turned and came back with a wooden case in her hand.

'These are what they came in,' she said, placing the case on a table. 'I'll take them down.'

She pulled a sofa away from the wall and placed a chair beneath the pistols, standing on it to reach above her and take down the pistols. She placed them in the case, the two nestling alongside each other in the velvet lining.

'I don't suppose he'll notice,' she said, speaking to herself as much as to Stephanie. 'He never comes in here anyway.'

Stephanie followed Mitzi back to the patio doors.

'You can go now,' Mitzi said, pulling the door open and standing with her hand on the latch. 'Lisa will be sorry to have missed you.' Stephanie nodded and stepped into the warm breeze. She raised her hand to wave but Mitzi had already slid the window shut and turned away.

Mitzi walked across the lounge and turned on the radio. A woman's voice wafted lazily into the room, *'Is your mouth a little weak, when you open it to speak?'*

The Essay

The gun was alive in her hand, its weight pulling her arm
so that she appeared like a figure possessed, skittering across
the hillside, the tragic heroine drawn toward the copse. She
stopped to gather herself, sweat pouring down her forehead,
blurring her vision. She raised the gun, slowly, the way a
gunman would, one eye closing, the movement synchronised.
The pistol was level with her eye now. She squinted along
her arm, along the length of her sleeve. The barrel of the gun
began to shake. Her arm sagged at the elbow, the gun swaying,
possessed. The dead weight of the pistol was too much, she
let it take her hand where it wanted to go, back to her side,
pointing once more at the ground, drawn by the earth's core.

Stephanie stood in the field, the wind blowing in from the
estuary cool on her face, the scar smarting, livid. A fine mist
of drizzle pushed up the valley, ghostly in the afternoon, like
a gauze over the land. Birds wheeled and scattered before it,
soaring high into the dark then banking and drifting away,
awakened by the change in the elements, black specks in the
void. Then the rain was upon her, softening her, moisture
settling in her hair, on her clothes.

The gun slipped from her hand, a gentle thud as its weight

was swallowed by the earth. She turned about, away from the rain, the wind behind her, and ran across the side of the hill, resisting the pull of the slope joining a path trodden by cattle or deer, the growth worn away by innumerable journeys.

She stopped once she reached the woods, panting, chest pounding, the water running down her face even though she was under the canopy of the trees. Bent double, holding herself tight, retching, the bile dripping from her mouth, the taste burning her throat. She wiped it away, smearing it on the sleeve of her jacket, leaving a trail that made her think of the snails and slugs that made for the doors of the house at night, evidence of their progress criss-crossed on the stones of the path.

The house was waiting for her, watching as she scurried through the sudden rain, seeking shelter. She paused at the door and remembered the gun. Its twin was in the attic. She took the stairs quickly, careful not to make any sound, avoiding the boards that she knew would creak. As she pulled down the attic ladder it emitted a screech, the scrape of metal so loud that she stopped dead, before testing her weight on the steps, cautiously transferring from one foot to the other as she made her way up and into the light at the top of the house.

The second pistol was where she had left it, in the bag that Garrick had passed to her. He had said that the case Mitzi had provided was too conspicuous and had given her a nondescript brown leather bag for the weapons. She took the gun out and held it in her hand, feeling the smooth round weight of the grip in her palm, too big for her hand, her delicate fingers wrapping around the butt of the weapon, stretching for the trigger. The metal underneath her fingertips was smooth and hard, cold. Gently she pressed, pulling it back towards her, feeling it resist and looked up at herself in the mirror, taking aim. A young man stared back at her, a questioning smile on his face. Her breathing stopped, her eyes widening. Was this Delmont? She squeezed harder, holding the trigger, feeling the tension as it hovered just at the point of letting the hammer fall, the figure swaying in her sights.

'It was given to me by Mr Howell, landlord of the Green Dragon Inn on King Street.'

She felt rather than heard the voice, calm and measured inside her head.

'Mr Howell's journeyman, William Hewlett, procured its pair from Partridge, the confectioner.'

Again her hand started to shake, the weight too much for her. Gradually, as if being winched down notch by notch, she lowered her arm, shaking with the effort. She dared herself to look in the mirror. The young man had gone, replaced by the girl with the scar and the grubby clothes. She sat down on the floor, cradling the gun in her lap. She would need a teacher.

The Lesson

The gun was still there, its nose stuck in the ground like a pig's snout snuffling through the earth. She pulled it out, feeling the ground holding on to it, not letting go. She poked her little finger into the end of the barrel, smearing away earth and grass, the cold metal smooth against the rough of her fingers. She held it out again, her arm straight, her breathing steady.

'Bang.' She said the word. Calm. No shouting, no emotion, no drama, just a simple bang. She lowered the gun, keeping her arm straight.

She had decided on a teacher. It would be Birch. She wouldn't tell him about the duel. He would find out when it was all over.

Mr Birch was easy to find, as easy as finding the weather or the seasons or the days of the week. He would be at his yard, first thing in the morning, last thing in the evening. Up with the birds, home for lunch, then off again with his dog, head down. Goodboy, that's what the dog was called, or at least that was the name he had earned, always sniffing for something, head down like his master but seeing everything, tail down but happy. Goodboy. It had made Stephanie laugh when she had first heard it, not thinking you could call a dog something that wasn't a proper name. Some people gave their dogs people's names – Ben or Billy or Daisy – but she decided that dog's names were best, the right thing. She'd feel silly, she thought, walking through the park shouting out someone's name, worrying that a Ben, a Billy or a Daisy might answer her.

'What if there was someone there called Ben?' she'd asked her mother. As usual, Muriel hadn't answered. Sometimes Stephanie wanted to shout at her, grab her, 'Why can't you hear me?' but there didn't seem any point. She must have her reasons.

'Goodboy, come here boy, come on.'

Birch was standing by his tractor in the rain, an elbow resting on one of the wheels as the skinny figure strode down the slope, past the barn and through the sheep, straight towards where Birch was waiting. The boy kept his head down, shielding himself from the rain perhaps, or because he didn't want to be recognised. Birch was a short man, built like the cattle he loved, big, solid Charolais, their parts fitting together like some primitive creation that defied the laws of physics and biology to function. Like his cows, Birch stood poised, leaning forward on his shins, as if ready to bolt or fall forwards to the ground. The bulk of his body, not immense but solid and full, leant a tremble of fragility to his legs, their spindliness accentuated by the mass they supported. Their length, though, was in proportion to that weight, invariably set apart, braced like the circus strong man at the foot of the human pyramid.

The boy stopped a few feet in front of him, short hair plastered to his head, a scar vivid down his face. Birch shivered.

'Hello, Mr Birch.'

Birch stood, waiting.

'It's me, Mr Birch. Stephanie. Matt's daughter, Stephanie.'

Birch coughed, a splutter erupting as if from a faulty engine.

'What you do that for, girl? I thought you were some young gun out to do me no good.'

Stephanie brought her hand up to her face, her hair.

'I cut it, Mr Birch.'

'That's not the only thing you cut, by the looks of it,' he said, his eyes following the jagged line of the scar. 'What you do that for?'

Stephanie ignored the question. She was in a hurry, she had decided. She liked Mr Birch. She did not, however, have time for small talk. She knew that if she ceded too much to Birch, she would be there for a good hour discussing the cows, the brother, the chickens, the state of various parts of fencing in the area, the recent movements of springs and any one of a hundred concerns that helped Birch sleep peacefully at night, lulled by nothing stronger than a pint of milk.

'I wanted to ask you something,' she said.

'Oh yes.' Birch's years at market had taught him a few things. He could size up a piece of livestock without even pausing as he walked past it in the pen, not betraying the merest flicker of interest. Even after the bidding the people around him wouldn't know that he had bought an animal. Only his brother would notice the discreet touches to collar or cuff that Birch used to signal to the auctioneer, the subtlety of his movements bearing the grace of the magician amid the frenzy of the market, animals and men competing to shout and stamp in their enthusiasm for the sale.

'I wanted to ask if you would teach me how to fire a gun.'

Birch paused. The skin above his eyebrows started to crumple, lines forming in the flesh. His eyes, though, remained sharp, small, dark points watching the girl.

'What was that?'

She repeated her request.

'Fire a gun?

'Yes, I need to learn how to fire a gun and you're the person who knows most about guns, Mr Birch. I thought if you taught me I could become a real expert, taught by the best.'

'I see.' Birch had learned other lessons in his time around animals. One such lesson was to avoid trying to understand what might motivate them, as it was likely that they would not know themselves.

He took off his cap and held it in one hand, wiping the back of his neck with it, a reflex he performed when he was at a loss. His brother, who was two years older but the one who generally made the effort to keep the house in order now that their mother was gone, had noticed this gesture and deduced that it had started off as the rather more natural movement of running his fingers through his hair, but as Birch's hair had receded and he had taken to wearing a cap to mask that retreat, so the movement had necessitated the removal of the hat with the hand that intended to run its fingers through his hair. Birch's hair, such as it was, now occupied a narrow band, an elongated tuft parallel to his neck and in line with his ears.

He put his cap back on, pulling it over his head, from back to front, in a manner that he had persuaded himself the ladies found to be somewhat dashing.

'I could do that,' he said. 'Reckon there's a few things I could teach you. Have to be careful, mind. Dangerous things, guns. Wouldn't want people knowing.'

Stephanie picked up her cue.

'No,' she said. 'No one will know. It will just be us.'

She followed him then, matching his pace, the rain still hanging in the air. Birch never walked quickly. Indeed, he seldom did anything quickly, as if he was pacing himself to last the day, each day a long course with the end visible from the start, far in the distance, until the last day which, as someone had once told him, would be shorter than the rest. There was little to be gained, he had reasoned, in hurrying.

They walked along the side of the long tin barn, holes and crannies along the rutted track filling up with water, puddles settling on the dark gold of the earth. They turned at the end of the barn and went to where some cattle were standing. She had never been here. This was where the brothers did their business, a dark place, barely decipherable to Stephanie as she heard rather than saw Birch open a door and disappear into the black of the inside.

He emerged a few moments later carrying a long stick wrapped in a dark cloth, a cloth that betrayed no colour in the darkness, the gloom robbing Birch too of any features, so he was merely a shadow holding a shadow. The shadow nodded at her, holding the shadow of the gun across itself with both hands, like a ghost bearing arms.

'We can go up to the old quarry, by the Rifleman's,' he said.

The Rifleman's had been a public house before anyone could remember, so long ago that nobody knew who it served, who the riflemen in need of refreshment had been. Behind it, up in the woods, was the quarry that had supplied the stone for the inn and many other of the local houses, as well as being a shooting gallery for the soldiers billeted in the town.

The rain had become heavier, lazier, the mist condensing into drops of moisture that gradually assumed more weight until they were falling with intent, hammering through the trees and striking the ground. Still Birch walked at his habitual pace, although Stephanie noticed that he moved to the sheltered parts of the track, in the way that an animal might intuitively find the path of least resistance. The rain was washing away the earth from the track, leaving the trail of stones and rocks uncovered, exposing the frame of the land, a mass of bone and cartilage that lay naked and washed. It was darker under the cover of the trees, the rain ushering in a softening of the day, a melancholy muteness spreading across the earth.

They climbed away from the track, Stephanie slipping on the mud of the bank, gripping the roots of trees to pull herself up. Goodboy was waiting for them at the top, panting, his tongue hanging out, blue eyes clear with excitement. They came into a meadow in the woodland fringed by hanging oaks and hazel, their branches weighed down by the moisture. At the far side of the clearing was a wall of rock, rough hewn, its dark edges fissured and cracked as if it had been part of a giant boulder that had been rent apart by some mighty blow thousands of years before. The forms of animals lay in these rocks, imagined figures glimpsed in the cut of the granite, the stones like blocks of teeth set upon square jaws the size of houses. The dark lowering mass of the rock face leant an unworldly air to the pale grass and moss that carpeted the clearing. There was no rain here, the air hung still, unruffled by the elements. Strewn on the ground were blocks of stone, as if scattered by giants, remnants of another age, another time. Beneath the wall sat the charred remains of a fire, a circle of stones set upon a broader round of ash.

The dog began to snuffle in the fire, its senses alert to the remains of food, tail wagging a frenzy of small circles until Birch called him over.

'Goodboy! Leave that now.' He turned to Stephanie, the gun still cradled in his arms. 'I reckon this would be as good a place as any. This is where me and the brother learned to shoot. There's still some holes in the wall there.'

Stephanie followed his eyes to the rocks, although she couldn't work out which marks in the intricate pattern of scratches and lines and chips that spread across the uneven surface of the rock might be the result of some boys learning to shoot half a century before.

Birch sat down on a rock, the dog following his movements as he removed the gun from its cover.

'It's special, this gun, Stephanie. There's not many like it. It's a bit like that dog there, Goodboy. A good gun and a good dog, I reckon, that's about all you might need.'

The gun was sleek, its long barrel thin like the bone of an animal, dark as ebony. The dull sheen of the metal was fitted to a rich wooden stock. Stephanie held her breath, willing herself to feel the tension, telling herself that she should remember this time, the time when Mr Birch took the gun from its cover and held it in his hands. She watched as he turned it over, handling the weapon with the same ease and familiarity he used with his dog. Goodboy sat watching his master, expectant. He knew this game, he knew about shooting, had been raised on shooting, knowing when to hold, waiting to hear his master's command, anticipating it, knowing it even before his master knew, hearing the change in his breathing, smelling the change as his master savoured the kill before releasing him to Fetch! Fetch! Stephanie waited, patient as Goodboy. Birch looked up at her, looked her straight in the eyes, as he would an adult. Satisfied, he nodded and rose from where he sat on the rock.

'Here,' he said, hands extending towards her, eyes down, not looking at her, looking away, out of deference, she thought, or decency. She even considered embarrassment, laughing to herself at the prospect. 'I reckon you could give him a go. See how he feels, like.'

She sat, patiently. She did not rise. She waited for Birch to bring the gun to her. He stopped, both hands reaching out to her, like an offering.

The gun was cold to her touch, a welcoming cold,

reassuring. She would not panic when feeling this. She slowed her breathing, eyes closed, her breath deep the way she could calm her nerves if she felt panicked. She felt the gun move in her hands and opened her eyes. Birch was looking at her, his hand on the barrel of the gun, forcing it down.

'Best make sure he's always pointing at the ground, Stephanie,' he said. 'Unless you want to shoot something, that is.' He laughed, a short laugh, aborted. She could sense him trying to gauge her intent.

'Rabbits, I expect.'

She looked at him, holding his gaze. It wasn't rabbits.

'No,' she said. Her voice trailed off. She thought about rabbits, about Easter hares boxing in meadows, duelling.

'It's not rabbits,' she said out loud. Birch nodded, taking his hand off the barrel of the gun and stepping back. Quickly, with a speed and decisiveness that surprised her, she raised the gun, pulling the barrel up with one hand, the other hand wrapping around the wood of the stock. She felt the trigger nestle intuitively in the fold of her index finger. She pulled it towards her, the butt hard on her shoulder.

'Bang!'

A click came from the hammer. Birch fell back, one step, then a second, his short legs buckling under his body like a steer felled, a hand stretching out behind him. He moved slowly, with something approaching grace, Stephanie thought. If she had to describe it to the police afterwards, she decided, she would definitely use the word graceful, or better still, balletic. He was balletic, officer, like a swan as he fell to his death. That was what she would say.

'Bang!' she shouted again. Then she laughed. Her own laugh was not a sound she was used to hearing.

Birch was sitting on the rock, his breath puffing out of him. She wondered if any of it had happened.

'Was that bad, Mr Birch?' she asked, her voice little again. 'I didn't mean to.'

He looked up at her. He had lost his cap in the fall and there was a handkerchief in his hand, not a very clean one. He brought it up to the dome of his forehead and wiped the clutch of material across, sweeping it from one side to the other.

Stephanie took a step towards him, the gun held level before her. Birch held his hand out, palm spread, as if in greeting. A nervous laugh, almost a death rattle, came from his mouth.

'Don't reckon you should ever point a gun at someone, Stephanie,' he said, 'even if he isn't loaded.'

Stephanie looked down at the rifle in her hands.

'No,' she said, her voice strong and determined. 'I'm sure you should not, Mr Birch.' She turned and nodded at the wall of rock, its tableau of living creatures frozen as if momentarily aware of a hunter. 'Now would you teach me how to fire the gun please.'

Birch laughed again, once more without a trace of mirth.

'Looks to me like you've already got an idea, Stephanie. Woman beyond your years, I should say.' He rose and took the rifle from her, watching the girl, not the gun. He broke the gun at the breech, smoothly, a well-oiled click the only noise. Holding it at arm's length he peered down the barrel. From the pocket of his coat he took a bright orange cartridge and inserted it, slotting it in, stubby fingers dainty with the precision of the movement. He clicked the barrel closed and held the gun in his two hands, considering its weight.

'Rabbits, birds, that's normally mostly what we use him for.' Birch said, as much to himself as to Stephanie. She watched him, admiring the way he fused himself with the gun, as if it was an extension of his body. He was still talking, telling her the way to turn, how to hold the butt of the rifle hard into your shoulder, how the recoil will be a shock, how it always is the first time. Without ceasing the patter of his speech he span in a graceful arc away from her, the gun coming up to his eyes as he turned to point up to the sky. Just at the point where the gun reached the apex of its trajectory a shot blasted out. Stephanie stumbled back, as if this time she had been hit, her mouth working to shout or scream, but even though she was sure she was saying something the only sound she could hear was the rushing of air, as if the soundtrack of the woods had been erased.

Birch was standing watching her, already reloading the gun, a smile on his face.

'Bit louder than your bang then, Stephanie.' He was laughing now, eyes still watchful under his cap. He held the gun out to her again. 'There you are then, take him. He's yours now.' He held on to the gun as she placed her hands on it, both of them holding the weapon. 'Careful mind, he's loaded.'

'Should I spin around, Mr Birch?' Her voice sounded strange in her head, muffled and distorted by the residue of the explosion.

'No, you don't need to do that. Just remember to hold him good and tight to your shoulder.'

She raised the weight of the gun, feeling the wood smooth against her cheek, and looked beyond it to the grey sky. Drops of rain fell on her upturned face. She tracked them as they arrowed down at her, her gaze picking one and following its trajectory until it was lost and she fixed on another, heavy, swollen with water. Her finger tightened on the trigger. She heard Birch behind her, telling her to squeeze gently, to feel the resistance. She could feel him close, sense his breathing as the shot rang out and the rain scattered from her view.

The Fitting

'Matthew?' She spat the word, the sound hanging in the darkness. 'Matthew!'

She looked at the mouth, agape, the tonsils swollen, swollen in his throat. His eyes were open but unseeing, as they always were when he slept. She wondered whether that was what his eyes would look like when he was dead. He turned over suddenly, wrapping himself in the cover, twisting himself like a baby held tight in the comfort of its swaddling. She pondered different ways of waking the sleeping baby: she could throw the covers back and shout 'Fire!' She could talk to him gently, try to lull him from sleep to wakefulness without any real transition, so that one was the continuation of the other and in the morning he would not know whether or not it had all been a dream. It would give him something to talk about when mother took him to see the psychiatrist, Stephanie thought, the one who had looked alarmed the time he had met Stephanie.

She shook his shoulder, then again, roughly.

'Up! Now!' She said the words, calmly, in a matter-of-fact way, letting his sleeping form know that there was no space for discussion, that this was what had to happen.

He opened his eyes fully, saw Stephanie and stared at her.

'Come on,' she said, 'there's something you have to try.'

She watched the struggle between body, eager to return to sleep, and brain, stirred, aware that it had things to do, a task to perform. His arm abruptly pushed the covers back, the too-young covers, pictures of diggers and tractors in bright colours, a relic of childhood.

'Why?'

She ignored him. There wasn't a 'why', she thought, not really. There was just an 'is', the thing they were doing, the thing they had to do. She didn't expect him to understand her need for respect, for recognition. Why should he? He was everything now.

He put his dressing gown on over his striped pyjamas, his feet in the slippers tucked neatly under the bed, and took his glasses from the bedside table. He followed Stephanie into the darkness of the landing, his hand reaching in the black, sliding up the wall to the light switch. Before he could find it, his hand flailing against the wall like a moth entranced by the light, Stephanie put her hand over his, pushing it away, back down to his side.

'Don't,' she whispered. 'It's more fun in the dark.'

'Stephanie.' He whispered too, but felt as if the words went no further than his lips, absorbed into the blackness.

She led him by the hand, her body inclining into the dark, confident in her blindness, him leaning back, as if being dragged down a steep slope. She stopped him by the ladder to the attic. 'Go on,' she said. 'Don't worry.' She sounded like the normal sister. She gently pushed him from behind, and followed him up, the two of them together on the ladder, something her father had warned them never to do.

She turned the light on, the single bulb casting an ineffectual yellow glow across the attic, and went to the trunk where she had put the uniforms she had got from Mrs Ripley's costume shop. The brass buttons gleamed up at her, even in the gloom, and her hand went out to touch them, her fingers feeling the cold brightness nestled in the soft red of the cloth.

She pulled out the two red tunics, one adorned with epaulettes, the other sporting three rows of gold braid across the front.

'This one is for you to wear,' she said, holding out the braided tunic to Matthew. He didn't move.

'What am I supposed to do with it?' he asked.

'Put it on. You have to wear it.'

He took the tunic from her, smelling the dust, the mustiness of age close in the still air of the attic. He slipped his hand into one sleeve, then the other, pulling the heavy jacket over his dressing gown. It hung off him.

'It doesn't fit,' he said. 'I don't want it.'

She looked at the jacket, its bulk making Matthew look puny, younger than his years, his fingertips protruding from the end of the sleeves as they hung down by his sides. It would have to do. She had it now and really the uniform was the least important part of it.

'Hold your arms out straight,' she commanded, 'as if you were holding a gun.' He did as he was told, his arm at 90 degrees to his body. He looked along his arm, closed one eye.

'We're not really going to do this, are we, Stephanie?'

She loved it when he sounded so young and helpless, so in need of a proper sister. It was just a shame, she sometimes felt, that she wasn't that sister. She was different. Surely he understood that.

'We have to do it, Matthew,' she said, trying to sound reasonable. 'It's unavoidable. We've said we'll do it so we have to, otherwise we would lose all honour.'

'But what if we actually get hurt? I mean, I know it's a game and everything, but still.' She thought for a moment she was actually going to laugh.

'Matthew,' she said, as if talking to a particularly slow-witted child, 'it's a duel.' She had the other jacket on now, and was doing up the rows of gold braid. When they were fastened she pulled the jacket down by its hem and puffed out her chest.

'Don't we look wonderful?' she asked him. 'Isn't this splendid?'

She stood in the attic, shoulders square, her back straight like a soldier on parade, her hair cut short, the vivid line drawn across her cheek. Matthew didn't answer.

'We should really have the right trousers,' she was saying, 'pantaloons, blue for you, grey for me. And gloves. Definitely gloves. They used to wear gloves. Every duel. White gloves, most often. The Germans had steel ones to protect their hands. Do you think Mother has some gloves?'

'Protect their hands?' Matthew echoed.

'From the sabre.' She made a slashing motion through the still air.

'Stephanie,' he said.

'Yes?' She was imagining the clash of metal on metal, of shouted commands, of honour satisfied.

'Can I go back to bed now?' The first light of dawn was coming through the window, a dull flat opening to the day bringing with it the tentative chorus of birds.

'What?' she said, not looking at him. 'Yes, if you want to.'

'Will it be soon, Stephanie?'

'Yes,' she said, 'very soon. I have the uniforms and the guns. Garrick will be the second, the doctor has said he will attend. There isn't really anything more that we need. We just have to wait for the day.'

She did look at him now, a boy in a jacket, still less than a man. The time between them was strange, she thought.

Sometimes it seemed as if years separated them, and she felt like his mother, protective almost, although those thoughts did not sit comfortably with her. She could appreciate that she was in charge, that he was her charge even if she was the younger sibling. Yet at other times, it felt as if he were her equal.

After Matthew had returned to the safety of his bed she made separate piles on the floor of the attic, one for her, one for him. She folded the tunics neatly, making sure they matched, with the collar open on view, the way they would be in a shop. Delmont was watching her from the mirror, a pipe in his hand, his white shirt unbuttoned. She looked behind her with a start but there was nobody there, the attic empty save for the boxes of books and a stack of chairs. She turned hesitantly back to the mirror but he had gone, the only trace of his presence a faint whisper of smoke and the smell of tobacco hanging in the air.

She laid a gun on top of Matthew's tunic, her hand shaking as she took it from the bag Garrick had brought. She almost dared not look as she was touching it. The dark metal of the barrel contained a menace she had not known before; it made her feel funny, and she had to sit down there on the floor, in the dust and dirt. The other gun lay in her lap, waiting for a command, waiting to carry out the task for which it had been created. It was almost time now. The two bullets were in the bag. Stephanie picked up one of the lead balls, rolling it around her palm, studying the texture of the dull, grey metal, the surface pitted and worn, each mark telling a story.

She would have to practise, although Garrick had said that as he knew how the guns worked he would load the bullets. He had paused when he had told her this, as if expecting a reply. They had been sitting in the same café, at the same table. He had placed the bag with the guns on the floor between them, and leaned towards her. He waited for her to reciprocate, to enter into the conspiracy, but she had remained sitting upright, refusing to play this game. So he remained, the curved 'S' of his body a feat of improbable mechanics, whispering as if he was telling a secret to a microphone buried in the bowl of sugar cubes in the middle of the table.

'I've brought the guns,' he had said. Instead of responding with some expression of curiosity she had merely regarded him with disinterest. 'The guns,' he said, the excitement spilling out of him. 'They're here, in the bag.' He nodded through the table at the bag lying on the floor between them. He wanted to get the guns out, to pull the bag up on to the seat next to him.

'I've checked them over,' he whispered. 'Quite remarkable. It's all there, powder, rods, bullets, everything. I wonder if Mitzi realised what she was giving you?'

The woman at the counter briefly looked up from her magazine to survey the strange couple in the corner, the older man and the young girl who seemed not to know each other.

'Will they work?' Stephanie asked.

'Absolutely. One may be a bit dicky, the mechanism looks a bit off. Might have a bit of a kick.' He sat back, beaming at Stephanie. 'I must say,' he said, speaking in his normal voice, 'this is the most terrifically exciting thing, Stephanie. What does your brother think? Is he looking forward to it as well?'

Stephanie looked at him as if he were mad, which, on consideration, she thought he might very well be.

'I don't know,' she answered. 'I haven't asked him.'

Garrick did not seem to hear. 'Gosh, he must be absolutely twitching with excitement,' he said. 'I know I would be. A duel! Imagine. En garde!' He was shouting again, although this time the waitress didn't even look up. 'Actually, I'm not even sure if you say en garde with pistols. Perhaps you just shoot first and apologise later.' He laughed at his joke, the flesh of his lips pulled back to expose an uneven row of large blackened teeth.

'Do you know,' he said, 'I've had an idea. What do you

think about doing the whole thing "au mouchoir"? It's the most thrilling way of duelling, something the French came up with, very creative.'

Stephanie waited, bored by Garrick's enthusiasm.

'The duellists stand facing each other and hold opposite corners of a handkerchief in one hand, a pistol in the other. Then they fire. It's absolutely compelling, and it removes any doubts about accuracy, so even if you're not confident about your aim you can be pretty sure you'll hit your adversary. What do you think? Worth a try?' He sat forward, poised like a dog waiting expectantly for a stick to be thrown.

'I'm going now,' she said. 'I need to sort things out.'

'Oh, yes,' said Garrick, his features dropping, 'of course. Absolutely. Sort things out. Definitely. Always things to be sorted out.' He leaned across the table again, like a character in a thriller. 'Do you want to take the bag?' he hissed.

She ignored him. Pulling her jacket over her shoulders she stood up and waited by the table as he extricated himself from the tangle of chairs and table legs, unruly limbs refusing to allow him to stand without knocking the table, which in turn caused the drink she had left behind to slowly topple over. The unfinished juice pooled on the table before finding its escape and trickling on to the carpet, narrowly missing the leather holdall.

'Oh dear,' he said, staring at the trail of liquid, frozen in his movement.

'I'll take the bag,' she said, picking it up, having to adjust her stance to allow for the weight of the guns. 'Bye, Garrick.'

The Appointment

Dr Sweeting was sitting in his chair when Stephanie entered the surgery. He wondered vaguely how she had managed to get in before the question drifted out of his mind.

'You look like you haven't moved, Doctor,' she said. 'I hope the shock of my last visit didn't kill you?'

He was not dead, although he was aware that his bones were increasingly calcifying, causing flashes of pain to spear along his limbs, leaving him breathless. His patients, themselves playing the part of the physician, would regard him with a mixture of fear and sympathy, and he had noticed a tailing off in their visits. Even most of his regulars had taken their ailments, imagined and real, elsewhere and he would sit for an entire surgery with just one or two patients. He had continued to assume the correct attitude for the ritual, the doctorly manner on which he had always prided himself had not deserted him, and had indeed become such a part of his nature that that he no longer knew where he, the old he, the real one, the one that had been there at the beginning, where he stopped and where the doctor began. It was not his manner, he felt sure, which betrayed the state of things to his patients. He tried to look around him, mentally, to see the surgery as others would see it, to itemise the elements that would suggest a practice gone awry, from the unruly scatter of books and papers on the desk, to the patina of dust that lay on the shelves, dulling the furniture. Perhaps the wastepaper basket brimming over with soiled tissues suggested a grander malaise. Dr Sweeting wondered about all these things but felt he was beyond caring, or that it was really too late in the day, too late in his day to care.

Although he had not been thinking directly about the girl or about her plans when she had walked in, she had been there in his mind, indeed had been in his thoughts since that last visit. Against his better intentions the prospect of the duel had sustained him in the intervening days. He had even sought out an account of the duel between Heazle and Delmont in a local history book written by a man who claimed to have met one of the unfortunate participants.

'I just came in,' she announced. 'There was nobody waiting.'

The doctor hurried to put his glasses on, swivelling his chair around to face the desk and assuming the posture of someone busy at his work.

'Ah, Stephanie,' he said, turning to face her and removing the glasses, 'and how are we feeling today?'

The girl frowned at him. 'That's not why I'm here, Doctor,' she said.

He paused, uncertain. He was sure she had come because she had an illness but he couldn't quite remember its nature. He decided to keep talking, hoping that it would all come back to him.

'And your mother? Is she well? Poor woman, I really must make the effort to get out to see her. I was only saying the other day... Was it to you? Well, you see.' Now he was quite lost. He was talking to himself, as if one of the imagined

120

conversations he so frequently conducted had emerged unchecked from his mouth.

'I'm sorry, what were we talking about?'

She turned to face him fully, exposing the gash across her cheek. He stared at the girl, his eyes flicking from the scar scything across her face to her eyes, his mouth moving soundlessly.

'It's a cut, isn't it?' he offered. He reached forward to better examine the patient but she moved away from his grasp.

'I've come about the duel,' she said.

Remembering, the doctor gathered himself, turning once more to his desk as if searching for some papers. 'Yes, yes, the duel,' he said. 'Tell me, how are the preparations? Have you identified the precise spot? I read an account, intriguing. It's important that you find the copse, and the weapons need to be authentic. Now, I had some thoughts about uniforms, no, not uniforms, hats! That's it, hats! Did you know that in the middle of the Napoleonic Wars the cocked hat was replaced by the stovepipe hat, except for the senior ranks? Now I assume our two duellists would have been wearing stovepipes, in which case we need to ensure that we have the right ones, with the correct amount of braiding to denote rank.' He looked up at the girl. 'Do you follow?'

She seemed to be suffering from a hot flush, her cheeks turning the red of the scar. The doctor carried on, becoming more sure of himself as he went over the details of the duel, telling her how the bullet had entered the unfortunate man through his side.

The girl, his patient, was growing increasingly agitated. Even as he was speaking he was aware that he had the makings of a rather advanced diagnosis of hysteria, if only he could keep in mind what he was talking about. Just as he was reaching a conclusion about the precise nature of the affliction striking the patient before him, Stephanie spoke.

'Dr Sweeting,' she pronounced, 'I can assure you that all the preparations are in hand, and that every effort has been made to ensure that the events will proceed as smoothly as possible. Indeed, most of the arrangements are now in the more than capable hands of my second, Mr Garrick...'

'Garrick Jeffries?' the doctor said. 'He used to be one of mine.'

Stephanie continued, denying the doctor the opportunity to reminisce about the curious case of Garrick Jeffries.

'As you can see,' she said, 'matters are quite advanced.' Her voice took on a calm, decisive tone, as if speaking from another age. 'All that needs to be done is to wait for the fourteenth of August, the date of the duel. You will need to be present at the appointed place at 6 p.m.' She got to her feet, her back straight.

Hearing the haughty tone and seeing her stand, the doctor felt obliged to follow suit, although normally he would remain seated once he had dismissed a patient. As he rose he felt a slight unsteadiness as the pressure in his blood responded to the movement. Stephanie held out her hand, arm straight.

'Goodbye, Doctor,' she declared. 'Until the duel.'

'Goodbye, young man,' he said. She turned abruptly on her heel and marched the three steps to the door and stepped out into the hallway, closing the door firmly behind her.

If she had looked back she would have seen the doctor standing as she had left him, motionless, staring at the space she had occupied in the room. As usual he was thinking about death, about his own death but also about the death of a young duellist.

The Mirror

She placed a gun on top of each of the tunics, the brown of the handles, polished and worn, offsetting the vibrant red fabric. The arrangement was a neat summary of the two beings who would shortly face each other, as if they had been reduced by some magical formula to nothingness, the substance of their existence removed to leave just the trappings, the clothes and the weapons, neatly folded in on themselves, empty vessels, symbols of what they had once contained. She laid a hand on each in turn, feeling their warmth and age, reaching for their histories and their stories. She didn't mind that the costumes were just replicas. Everything had its story, every fibre told a tale. She moved the gun from one of the tunics, setting it down on the attic floorboard, careful not to let it make a sound, as if the only sound it should make would be the last sound. She took the tunic in both hands and shook it loose of its folds, raising herself to hold it against her body. She turned to look in the mirror, its glass pitted with age but still offering enough of a reflection to make out her form. She saw the young man in the glass as if looking through time, his visage barely distinct, his posture erect. Through the dirt of the glass she could make out his gaze, hard, dark eyes looking back at her, his hair ragged, and burning bright across the picture, bleeding out of this vision, a welt of red across the face, the vivid scar that marked this man out for what he was: a duellist.

'I'm not doing it, Stephanie. I'm just not.'

She hadn't heard her brother climb the ladder. How long had she been staring at the mirror? She had always been fascinated by her reflection, had never been able to pass a mirror without pausing to inspect its contents, yet she did not consider herself vain. Indeed, her mother, when her mother had been interested in such things, had often said to her that she should care more for her appearance. One day all the mirrors had disappeared, removed from the house. Nobody said anything, it was not announced, but she knew that it must have been because of her mother. This had been shortly after her father had gone, when it had become just the two of them and her.

'I'm not doing it,' Matthew said. She looked at him through the mirror, the reflection of the soldier turning its head to regard the brother. Delmont's image was barely present in the glass, a shadow, a flicker at best. There was no life in him, she thought. The figure in the mirror spoke to Matthew in its voice.

'You're already doing it, Heazle. It has already started.'

She watched Delmont and felt a thrill at the authority he exuded. She turned to look at Matthew herself, smiling now as she saw the panic in his eyes, his resolve already crumbling. Her brother returned her gaze, uncomprehending.

'What if something goes wrong?' he asked.

She looked down at him, at this little boy who was older than she.

'Wrong? How can there be wrong? There isn't right or wrong, just simply what happens, what has to happen. You've read the story, or have you forgotten?'

The Eve

She stayed in the attic that night, listening to the house, sensing Delmont around her. The moon cast a cool opal light through the high window. In the mirror she observed the soldier preparing for the next day's duel, pacing back and forth, folding and refolding the same pile of clothes, checking the contents of the black valise: pistols, powder, lead balls, ramrod. Then he was gone.

She stood before the mirror and looked into her own eyes. Even there she saw retreat, reluctance. Was she brave, she wondered? What if she went to the appointed place and was unable to lift her pistol for the shaking of her hand? Would she be laughed at? Would her brother mock her? She knew that the next day she could be dead, that there would be no opportunity to hide or to flinch, that she would stand exposed before the consequence of the situation that she had chanced upon in the very room in which she was standing.

The night was interminable, the once-familiar sounds of the house, its groans and creaks, causing her to start in alarm, to look about her. Although she did not remember doing so, she must have fallen asleep several times, for she awoke with a jolt on more than one occasion, her head clouded with visions of sword fights, sabres flashing in the dawn light, guns held aloft awaiting the command to shoot, of lead balls and dropped handkerchiefs.

Twenty paces, fire on command, weapons to be raised and aimed and not lowered. Exchange of shots to continue until one party is seriously wounded.

She took a pistol from the bag and held it at arm's length, but the gun had a will of its own, waving erratically around the attic as if propelled by a magnetic force. She looked down the barrel, wondering if she could see death in the darkness of the small, deep hole.

She considered Delmont and Heazle, and how the events of that day in another age had led two friends to a mortal fight, apparently unaware of the likely outcome. Were they not frightened? Did they not have doubts?

Her body trembled in the chill of the summer night, a vibration extending along her arms and down her legs, causing her to lie down once more and cease her pacing. She wrapped her shivering frame in the scarlet tunic, feeling it coarse against her face, the smell of death around her.

Once more Delmont was before her, watching from the mirror. The box of papers was where she had left it, the contents undisturbed since she had extracted the story of the duel. She took it in her hands, feeling the soft fragility of the paper, the creases fraying, turning to dust in her hands. There was solace in the words, in the faded sprawl of the handwriting blurring in and out of legibility. Delmont paced back and forth as she read the story of his demise.

She had brought ink, pen and paper from her father's desk, its contents untouched since his departure. Spreading the paper out on the floor before her, she began to write, dipping the pen in the bottle of ink.

I, Lieutenant Joseph Francis Delmont, of His Majesty's 82nd Regiment, being of sound mind and body, do hereby attest that this is my last will and testament, written this night, the thirteenth of August. To my mother and my brother I leave the consequence of their actions, for only through the knowledge that they have forced me to defend my honour will justice be served and I will take my rightful place in the family. Troubled as I am by melancholy thoughts I know that I was not responsible for the loss of my father. Although I think of my life with revulsion you should understand that I have been but a child playing childish games. These games may have spilled beyond my world but that has not been my intention. Even so I have been judged. Such judgement has been an unbearable burden, but now I have found justice. When you remember me, do not celebrate. There shall be no music. There shall be no prayer. You may salute me as I pass, a soldier who died with honour.

Delmont put the pen down and looked at his reflection, an expression of calm satisfaction on his face.

The Casket

Stephanie spent most of the next day, the day of the duel, labouring in the attic with hammer and nails to fashion a suitable box from the planks she had carried up from her father's workshop. Beneath her the empty house creaked and sighed its way through the day, the stillness punctuated by her hammering, the noise ricocheting through the house like gunshots.

The box didn't feel right, although she wasn't really sure what it was supposed to feel like. She lay herself down in it, feeling the sides pressing against her, too tight, too narrow at the shoulders. She wondered if it would take her weight when they lifted it, whether she would be heavier then or lighter. She pulled herself up out of the box and looked down at the construction. She wondered if she should make one for Matthew as well, just in case, or whether this one would be big enough for him. Just in case.

Her effort was pitiful. One side was slightly longer than the other, meaning that the whole assemblage looked like one of those nonsensical shapes she had to study at school, a rhomboid or a parallelogram.

She decided that she would summon Matthew to help her.

Sometimes when she thought about something really hard it would happen. Usually it wasn't anything particularly useful, but still, it was something. She thought about Matthew, picked up the hammer and banged it on a piece of wood, insistently, the rhythm steady, like a drum calling a soldier to battle. She knew it would draw him, make him come and investigate, summon him home.

She did this for a while and then stopped. The house seemed to breathe a sigh of relief, although Stephanie could still hear the echo of the banging. It ceased and was replaced by a dull pain in the middle of her forehead. There was no Matthew. She had another idea. She would go outside and wait with the hula-hoop. This normally worked, although she was never sure if it was because it had an effect or because she was simply there for so long that at some point the thing she was willing to happen would be bound to occur.

She climbed down the ladder and went into the garden, setting the hula-hoop on its lazy twirl around her waist, looping now quicker, now slower. She stood still and watched it spiral gently, lazily down her thighs, descending her blue leggings before she rescued it again, bringing it back up to her waist, her midriff, her stomach, her chest.

She saw him before he appeared, looked to see him come around the corner and imagined him a fraction of an instant before he was there. The reality of Matthew coming around the corner was less vivid than her imagining of it. There was nothing about it, just a boy on his way home. She was pleased though. She had thought about him and he had appeared. She liked these things. She carried on twirling the hula-hoop, wondering if he would notice her or acknowledge that he had seen her.

She called to him, the hula-hoop taking care of itself, as if it would continue spinning were she to step outside of its circle.

'Hi Matty!' She had wanted to be light, carefree, but he hated it when she called him Matty. It usually meant that she wanted something.

'What do you want?'

'I need your help.' She realised that the words sounded desperate, alarming. 'It's in the attic.'

He went into the house, dropping his bag on the floor. Stephanie followed close, edging him along the way you would herd an animal without it being aware of what you were doing. As they reached the metal steps, she pushed ahead of him, holding the rail and springing up the ladder, enjoying the clank as she pulled herself up.

'Here,' she announced. Matthew's head was just appearing through the hatch. 'What do you think?'

She stood aside to let him see the results of her labour.

'What's it for?' Matthew asked.

She looked at him, wondering if he really didn't know.

'Matthew.' She sounded like her mother. Sometimes it just happened that her mother's tone was the only one to adopt for certain conversations, certain speeches or sermons. 'Isn't it obvious?' He was staring blankly at her, his default posture when the world did not make sense.

She waited, watching as his mind worked to understand precisely what was being asked of him.

'Matthew,' she barked, 'what does it look like?'

He squirmed, biting his lip, twisting the forefinger of one hand between the thumb and forefinger of the other. It reminded her of the times when he had been little and they were out somewhere and he had been so desperate to go to the toilet but afraid to ask, and had stood with one leg crossed over the other, feet entwined.

'You have to help me make it,' she said.

She took a step towards him, ignoring the way he flinched.

131

'You try,' he said.

She led him to the box, placed her hand on his shoulder and pushed him firmly down. He tried to spin away but she had hold of his arm.

'Let go,' he said, the beginning of panic in his voice, as if he were unsure whether to be frightened or not. 'Let go of me.'

She kept hold, pushing him down until he was sitting in the box.

'That's it,' she said, as if tucking him in for bed. 'Here, let me take your glasses.' She unhooked his spectacles from one ear and peeled them away from his face. 'Now lie down and we'll see if it fits you.'

Matthew was trembling. She could feel the vibrations through his arm. She decided to ignore it.

'Right, now let's get your legs down there,' She pulled his legs down, like a nurse in a very important clinic. 'That's very good. Now just lie back.' She hardly had to push him at all. It was more a case of simply easing him back into the box, helping his body recline.

It seemed to fit him quite well. In fact, it might have been made for him. He had closed his eyes.

'Matthew,' she said, softly, 'you don't have to close your eyes. You're not dead yet.' She laughed at her joke. People would say that she had a good bedside manner, she thought. Matthew would remember. He would tell them. 'She was very kind,' he would say.

Matthew opened his eyes so wide it was as if he could not see anything, could not get enough light into them. He opened his mouth, and screamed.

At first Stephanie didn't realise what was happening. She had been so enjoying herself, playing nurse and patient in a way that they hadn't done for years, in fact had never done, that she was confused by the high-pitched sound. She could see his small teeth and the little white spots on his red tongue, noticed them, catalogued them, before her brain turned to the noise that seemed to be coming out of this cavity. She could not make sense of it.

For a moment, Stephanie wondered if he were possessed, and if he were, whether it would be a good possession, like the sort when people in churches became so close to the Lord that they actually passed out, or whether it would be more like the sort of possession where the Devil crept into the body through some unlikely orifice and infected the entire soul.

Matthew stopped screaming while Stephanie was thinking about all of these things, and closed his eyes.

'Matthew,' she said, 'are you alright?'

She suspected he was going to start screaming again, that the pause had only been in order to get his breath back. She could even hear the noise, even though he hadn't started. Instead, he opened his eyes, looked at her, looked around at the attic, and with unlikely speed and even agility, jumped out of the box, causing Stephanie to lose her balance from her position crouching at his side. Matthew was already at the steps, hurling himself down through the hatch, the metallic clanging of the ladder ringing through the house.

The Witness

At the appointed hour, Stephanie went to find her adversary. Matthew was in the chair in the sitting room, the book open in his lap, one hand scratching furiously at his chest through his shirt. She disliked everything about this room: the heavy floral curtains, the green carpet and the absurd Arabian rug her mother had bought. He did not look up when she came in, refusing to acknowledge the intrusion into his realm.

'Come on,' she said. 'It's time.'

He ignored her, as he always did when reading his book, as if she didn't matter.

'Matthew!' She used her strident voice. 'We can't be late. Garrick's waiting for us.'

He heard this, as she knew he would.

'Who's Garrick?' he said, his voice drowsy.

'Garrick?' she answered, mimicking his tone. 'Garrick is the second, Matthew. We have to have a second.'

'A second?'

He raised his head from the book to look at her.

She was wearing the uniform, pantaloons tucked into a pair of knee-high black boots, the red tunic with gold braids across the chest, a black hat on her head, his uniform in one gloved hand, a small black valise in the other. She was standing straight, her shoulders stiff.

She placed the bag on the floor and strode towards him, for once snatching the book from his hands, feeling the coarse cloth on its cover, closing it before he could remonstrate with her.

'You need to get dressed. It's time to go.'

'Do we have to do this, Stephanie? I'm in the middle of my book.'

She ignored his question and thrust the other uniform at him. Reluctantly, he stood and shook out the tunic, pulling it over his shirt. Then he hopped around the room, first taking off his trousers, then threading his legs through the blue pantaloons and squeezing his feet into the boots.

When he had finished she made him stand before her, inspecting him in the way officers inspected soldiers on the parade ground. She raised a hand to brush some imaginary dust from his shoulder, taking pleasure in the way he flinched.

They left the house and walked up the lane towards the woods, a keen light bathing the valley in the late afternoon, lending a stillness to the fields around them. They came once more to the entrance to the field they had passed through when they had first visited the copse.

'We need to wait here,' she said softly. Matthew moved his head, barely acknowledging her presence, and they leaned against a wall, feeling the warmth from the soft stones through their thick clothing. Stephanie walked up the lane a little to see if Garrick was waiting. A few yards further on a barn stood, its green corrugated metal doors warning away intruders. A pair of house martins flitted around it, arcing and skipping through the sky.

Heazle and Delmont were seen sitting on a low wall, playing with a dog, waiting for Sargeaunt; and perhaps intending thereby to divert attention from the serious purpose on which they were intent.

In the distance a tall figure could be seen striding up the hill, at first just the tip of a black top hat visible, the brow of the hill edging down the body to reveal a long black coat with white buttons over drab-coloured trousers and black boots. Stephanie recognised Sargeaunt from the description on the wanted poster. He was carrying a small black travel bag, swinging it from his hand as he strode along the lane.

By the time he reached them Garrick was sweating, perspiration trickling down his face tracing small rivulets along the creases in his skin, his cheeks crimson, his dark-framed spectacles opaque with condensation.

'What a wonderful afternoon, absolutely charming.' He stood beaming at Stephanie, chest heaving, infinitely pleased with himself. 'Is this the right spot? I do hope I'm not late. I took the liberty of following the description, thought it only right I should dress for the occasion.'

Belatedly, he noticed the slight figure behind Stephanie.

'Ah-ha!' he pronounced. 'This must be the brother, the fearsome duellist! Hello! Hello! I'm Garrick, terrific to meet you.' He moved towards the terrified boy, one hand extended.

'Matthew doesn't really like people touching him,' said Stephanie, adopting her mother's voice. 'Do you, Matthew?'

Garrick was unperturbed.

'Right-ho, no harm done. On we go.' He opened the bag that he had set down before them. 'A change of clothes for you, Matthew, for afterwards.' Inside were a black coat, a striped waistcoat and a rather crumpled black top hat. 'All the rage in the nineteenth century, you know,' he said.

Matthew looked like he was going to be sick.

'Why do I need that?' His voice was high, a little boy again.

'It's for the getaway,' Garrick whispered, as if imparting a great secret to a co-conspirator. 'So we can spirit ourselves away into the night. Don't want to look like military men, do we?' Garrick appeared delighted with his role.

'I must say you two are quite the part,' Garrick said, looking them up and down. 'Those tunics truly look like the real thing.'

'Sargeaunt!' The curt tone in Stephanie's voice cut across Garrick's babbling. 'Did you bring everything?'

He seemed taken aback at the interruption, offended almost at the suggestion that he might have overlooked something in his preparations.

'Why of course, everything, absolutely.' He emphasised the words, leaving Stephanie in no doubt. 'I have all the additional items that Mrs Plommer was so kind to provide. There will be no omission.'

Stephanie nodded, satisfied. She could hear her heart beating under the heavy tunic, the blood thumping in her head.

'Come on,' she said.

The three figures, clad in antique clothing like a band of travelling players, climbed over the stile and followed the path as it swept down the hillside. The colours had changed since Stephanie and Matthew had last been there. The field now was parched, summer's long heat having sapped the life from it. The grass was wispy, ruffled by the breeze.

They could see into the trees, soft light illuminating the hues and forms inside the dense woodland. Through the dappled light, in the soft shadows of the woods, where colour and shape seemed to dissolve, Stephanie spied a movement. She held her gaze on the path, not slowing or speeding up, but all the while keeping watch to the side. After a few steps she saw it again, a body flicking through the branches, its stealth and sense of purpose betraying a human form rather than an animal. Ahead she could see a small break in the fence, a gap in the barrier that separated path from woods. As she reached it she turned, without slackening her pace and with no indication to the others. They stopped in their tracks, Garrick almost falling over Matthew, so sudden was the change of course. She gestured behind her for them to be quiet and plunged into the dark of the woods, her feet barely making a sound as she moved across the dry ground. She had seen a movement, she was sure of that, certain there was a figure tracking the three of them. Now that she was in the gloom, she was not so sure. Deeper inside the woods it was as if some natural disaster had struck. The trunks of trees lay slumped against each other, giant roots pulled up without ceremony. Stephanie found herself clambering over trunks, branches flicking at her when she passed.

She approached a large oak where she was sure she had last seen the movement. As she drew closer she could make out the marks on the tree, carvings, smatterings of messages and words, symbols hacked into the bark, a rough image of a gun.

'I'm over here, Stephanie.' She turned with a start to the voice. It had come not from the tree but from behind her. Birch was standing looking at her.

'Seen you coming down here. Thought I'd take a look, not being nosy, mind.' He gave a little laugh.

'Hello, Mr Birch. We're just out for a walk, my brother and a friend of ours.'

'So I see.' His gaze lingered on her clothes, the tunic with the braid and the buttons, the black bag in her hand. 'Interesting hat your friend's wearing there,' he said. 'Don't see many top hats in this day and age.'

'We're rehearsing a play, Mr Birch, for the historical society. We thought it would be better if we came out here to do it in the open, away from prying eyes.' At this she raised her eyes to look Birch squarely in the face, summoning all her courage. He looked back at her, his pale blue eyes blinking once, twice, blank like his cattle. He nodded his head.

'Right you are then, Stephanie. Long as everything's as it

should be. I'd better be on my way in any case, got cows to move.'

Afterwards, when it was all over, he would try to remember exactly what had happened in the woods, what she had said, the expression on her face.

The Duel

They walked across to the copse, the three of them in single file following the line of bare earth slanting across the field, Stephanie leading, unseeing, instinct alone guiding her, fingers trailing through the purple tips of the long grass. Matthew followed, his head bent to the ground as if he were climbing an incline. At the rear came Garrick, drunk on the atmosphere, exclaiming to himself all the while, proclaiming the beauty and clarity of the situation.

The group arrived at the copse, the dense vegetation giving way to sparse cover, the trees around the edge standing thin and forlorn, a guard of honour at a funeral.

The procession went clockwise around the copse, circumnavigating almost its entire perimeter, as if abiding by some ancient order of things, following the sun before they came to an opening that allowed them to scramble through, their heavy tunics catching on the thorns.

Inside, the air was cooler, the heat of the day having failed to penetrate the circle of trees. Stephanie looked at the soft, untrodden grass, considered the spindly trees lining the inside of the copse, the yellowing bracken curling in on itself as it endured the throes of its death and decided that this might have always been a place of sacrifice, a killing ground.

The three paused, unsure of the next step. Stephanie knew that she could not let the moment pass, that she must hurry in case Matthew tried to run away. Before she could place the protagonists in their positions, with a flourish Garrick produced a sheet of paper from his bag.

'I took the liberty of bringing some ground rules with me,' he said. 'I am the second, after all.' Stephanie could feel the heat rise through her face, a hot flush spreading from somewhere in her chest, annoyance at the intrusion tickling her. Garrick cleared his throat and began to read.

'The Code of Honour,' he declared, his voice ringing around the circle as he turned to address the audience of trees arranged around him. 'Firstly, the first offence requires the first apology, though the retort may have been more offensive than the insult.'

He cleared his throat and continued reading. 'Secondly, if the parties would rather fight on, then, after two shots each, the offended party may explain first and the offender apologise afterwards.'

'Garrick,' Stephanie tried to interrupt him, but Garrick was enjoying the sound of his voice in the trees, the sense of occasion, the majesty of the event.

'Thirdly, if a doubt exists who gave the first offence, the aggressor must either beg pardon in express terms, exchange two shots previous to apology, or three shots followed by explanation or fire on till a severe hit be received by one party or the other.'

'Garrick,' she said again, her voice rising.

'We're not actually going to shoot anything, are we?' They had both forgotten Matthew, who had been sitting on the ground watching the insects labouring up the long blades of grass.

Stephanie ignored him and turned to Garrick. 'We don't need to hear all of this,' she said. 'We know what to do, we've been through it. Let's just get on with it.' She stared at him, waiting to see if he would challenge her. Stories flitted through her mind of seconds being challenged during a duel, of their role in the proceedings giving offence to one of the duellists.

'Oh, gosh,' Garrick said. 'I'm sorry, I thought it might help to lay out the rules.'

'We don't need them, Garrick. I've read the story. I know what happens.'

He took the pistols out of the bag and began the business of loading them. First he took a thin metal rod and pushed it down the barrel. Then, he carefully tipped a quantity of black powder from a pouch into the barrel before laying a small square of material over the end of the upturned gun. Like a magician, he produced the round bullet, the lead dull and deadly, and placed it on the material before pushing it into the barrel with the metal rod. He cocked the pistol, a single click, and lay it on the ground, before turning to its twin to repeat the process.

Stephanie paced around the clearing, picturing the arena, imagining where they would stand, judging the position of the sun, the position of the second. She braced herself, feeling the unfamiliar stiffness of the tunic, imagining herself on a parade ground. Her mind flickered to what was about to happen, to the physical reality of what was about to happen. Would it hurt, she wondered? Would she feel anything? She had cut her leg once when she was little, sliding through the mud only for a piece of flint to slice into her leg. She had got up and run on, oblivious, pausing moments later to rest her hands on her knees, to draw breath, and then, there, to see the blood pouring down her shins and into her shoes. Then she had found herself sitting down, seeing the gash on her leg, the white of the bone showing through the parted skin, and only then had she felt the pain, had the parts of the puzzle come together in her mind to help her understand that she had a cut and that the blood was coming from a wound that she could only now comprehend.

Would it hurt, she asked herself, holding her sides, as if to stop the bleeding. She thought about the bullet, about how far the lead would travel into her, through her. Would she run screaming from the woods? Or would she succumb, falling to the ground with a sigh? There was no record of Delmont as he received the wound, of whether he had cried out or had fallen meekly like an animal, a deer startled as it stood, its legs buckling, to sink to the earth.

Matthew was watching her, his eyes round through his glasses, following this strange figure as it paced around the clearing, counting and muttering to itself, the livid scar on its face shouting across the silence.

'Why are we doing this, Stephanie?' His voice sounded small, even to him. He spoke again, raising his voice as much as he dared. 'Stephanie, why are we doing this?'

She strode across the grass to stand before her brother, legs akimbo, hands on her hips, and looked down at him, pathetic in the grass.

'Honour, Matthew,' she said, the scar even more violent on her face, transforming her. 'Justice.' Her voice was gruff, the voice of a soldier. 'Stand up,' she commanded. He brought himself to his feet, his body heavy as if pinned to the warmth of the ground. She shook him by the shoulders.

'Matthew,' she said, her voice now quiet but menacing. 'We are going to stand back to back, Garrick will tell us when to walk and will count out the paces. Before I have taken my sixth pace, you turn and shoot straight at me and if you don't I will turn and shoot at you.' He flinched, as if she had hit him, and tried to squirm out of her grasp.

'So I turn around and squeeze the trigger and shout bang, like when we practised?' he asked.

'Matthew!' She shouted at him now, her control momentarily leaving her, the flush rising once again on her cheeks. She breathed out, forcing the air out of her, feeling it leave her body. 'You will shoot at me.' She stood back, letting go of his shoulders, looking at the small, frightened face. He was trembling, his lip quivering. She wanted to laugh at him, to sneer, but she restrained herself. That would not be right, she thought. It would be ungentlemanly. At times like this, she knew, she should act correctly. She knew that it was incumbent upon her to remain calm and sanguine, to put emotion to one side and to observe the utmost respect for the ceremony and for her adversary. She focused again on Matthew, trying to apply the principles she had just enumerated to the boy in front of her. She let go of his shoulders and he slumped, flopping back to the warm embrace of the grass.

Her sight was drawn by the distant call of a buzzard, circling in the sky. Inside the clearing everything was still, as if time had suspended itself.

Garrick walked to the centre of the clearing, placed the top hat on his head like a judge preparing to deliver sentence, swept his frock coat behind him to reveal a striped waistcoat and cleared his throat.

'Gentlemen,' he began, his voice plummy as if he were addressing a meeting. 'We have come here to address a matter of the utmost seriousness, a slight that if allowed to pass uncorrected would have the most profound repercussions for both the friendship of these two fine officers and for the very honour of their respective regiments, of the town and indeed of His Majesty's Army—'

'Garrick!' Stephanie barked at him. She pulled Matthew up and the two of them joined Garrick. 'We're ready,' she said quietly. 'Garrick, before we are disturbed.'

'Absolutely, yes, I agree entirely, before we are disturbed,' he echoed.

'You need to get the guns,' she said. They waited while he retrieved the two loaded pistols, carefully pointing them at the ground as he walked towards the duellists.

'Right, now, here we are,' he said as he reached them. 'Which one would you like?' It was as if he was offering a plate of biscuits at a children's tea party.

Stephanie reached for one of the pistols. She had made Garrick tell her which one had the better mechanism.

It was a horse-pistol that had belonged to one of the volunteer cavalry, and is said to have been foul and rusty.

'Matthew, this one is yours,' she said, handing the second weapon to her brother.

This pistol was similar to the other, but was clean and in better condition.

'Remember,' she said, looking at the boy's downcast face, 'the trigger is very sensitive.' She closed his fingers around the weapon, making him grip it, and removed her own hands. He looked down at it in surprise, as if startled to find himself holding a loaded gun.

'Now,' said Garrick, 'when you shoot, keep your body side on and gently squeeze the trigger. If you jerk it you will pull your shot. And keep your hand steady.' Stephanie walked the few paces to the centre of the circle, turning herself to face the early evening sun, feeling its warmth recede. A breeze brushed across her face and the trees in the woods swayed, their forms echoing the wind. Garrick led Matthew to her, turning him around, the pistol limp at the boy's side.

The two figures stood back to back, bright dashes of colour in the soft evening light, the colours of their jackets vivid against the pale grass. All was quiet, the moment suspended, the air still.

'One!' From nowhere, Garrick's voice shouted out. Matthew moved forward with a jerk, as if he had flinched. Immediately Stephanie felt the space between them, the cool air against her skin. She stood, teetering, pressing on her toes to stop herself from falling.

'Two!'

The sound rolled across the hills and into the valley. A murder of crows rose as the word reached them, as if a breeze had buffeted them up.

'Three!'

Garrick was going too fast. She wanted to stop him, to shout at him, 'Slow down! It can't pass this quickly!' But she knew she couldn't, that she would break the rules, that she would lose face. She wasn't sure if she had stepped forward when he had called out the last number. She wasn't even sure what the last number had been. She tried to think, but before she could retrace the count in her mind Garrick called again.

'Four!'

There was a rhythm now, the numbers assuming their own pace.

'Five!'

Matthew stepped forward again, his feet meeting, as if standing to attention on a parade ground, his shoulders back. Stephanie had not taken the last step, had not been able to move her feet, despite willing them to take a stride. She almost cursed in annoyance, frustrated at her inability to control her own body. Even her breathing was beyond her control, coming in gasps, the thin air wafting through in warm waves, washing over her. She began to feel dizzy, to sense the ground coming towards her. Why had Garrick not shouted the next number? Had he stopped counting? She was sure that the next number would be six.

Still she did not take a step. She thought that if she did manage to move she would run from the clearing, but she could not. She looked down at the gun in her hand. Behind her she heard the sound of Matthew moving, yet she had not heard Garrick call out the next number.

She tried to turn, forcing her body to twist around to her left, her feet heavy, as if already buried in the ground.

When the bullet came, it was as if she had been dealt a blow by a hot shard, an intense pain in her side followed immediately by a shove, pushing her to the ground to leave her gasping not from the pain but from the heat that seemed to be taking the life from her, sucking away her energy, draining her. The grass pressed into her cheek, the smell sweet, dreamy, a smell of her childhood, forcing her back to her mother, to the very earliest of days. The sun came into view, pivoting to catch her in the face, her eyes staring at it as it moved across the sky, rolling around to greet her. She felt her legs twitching, while around her there was movement, footsteps through the earth, the heat in her side spearing her, twisting inside, burning its path into her body. She tried to close her eyes, to will herself to stop her feet twitching but found that her eyes too were beyond her control, that even as she tried to force them shut they remained fixed, glazed. Her head, she knew, was too heavy to raise, its weight forcing her face down into the ground, pinning it down.

She had heard Garrick shout but then there had been silence. Had she been shot? Had her brother turned and pointed the gun and pulled the trigger as she had told him to? She wondered if this was part of the story, if she should be lying here, her face pressed into the warm earth, if Heazle and Sargeaunt had deserted her and she was alone here in this copse. She could not feel her stomach, could not feel pain nor any sensation. She wanted to raise herself to see, or to move her hands to feel the wound, to feel if there was a wound, but she was pinned to the ground, helpless.

She saw Garrick standing in front of her, crouching down, his face staring into hers, his mouth moving fast, excitedly, eyebrows dancing about his forehead, spittle flying from his lips. There was a hand on her shoulder and she was rolled, the horizon wheeling up and across the sky. Garrick filled her view, his face grotesque, reddened, his hand pressing on her body. She opened her eyes and he fell away, his face replaced by Dr Sweeting, Birch behind him, leaning in, his breath fast.

The doctor found Sargeaunt supporting Delmont, who was on the ground, bleeding profusely from a wound in his left side. A ball had passed through his body; and Mr Sweeting, on probing the wound in his chest, at once declared its dangerous character.

It was as if she were watching a mime. She could follow what they were saying even had they not been speaking. She remembered the silent films her father had made her watch when she was little, the characters gesticulating and sighing at the slightest provocation. She looked dumbly at the doctor as his hands pressed on to her, concern furrowed into his face.

The Handcart

When Stephanie awoke she was being bounced in a cart across the hillside, traversing the same path she had traced so many days before. She was in a wheelbarrow, Birch pushing, looking down at her the way a parent might look at a baby in a pram, the doctor alongside him.

Dr Sweeting had prepared for this moment with great care, stationing his medical bag just inside the surgery door so he would know where it was when the time came and would not leave without it. Several times in the intervening days he had looked at the bag in puzzlement, wondering why it had been left in such an odd place, stooping to pick it up only to pause, aware that somewhere in the back of his mind he knew it had been placed there for a reason.

When the day came, it had not been forgetfulness that had made him miss the appointed time. He had read the account and knew that the doctor would not come until he had been summoned by the witness. He had been able to avoid having to make the decision to leave, to climb the hill to take part in a ceremony against his calling. So he had sat in his surgery, watching the hands of the clock, dozing through the afternoon until he was woken by the report. It had not taken long after that. He thought about Stephanie, how she had come to him in need. He had been waiting since then, waiting for this time, the possibility of escape it offered, the thrill of being central to a life, of being able to decide, to take and to give.

He heard the door open, had imagined hearing the footsteps pounding down the pavement and up the path to the door. Birch burst through the door and pulled the doctor up by his arm.

'Come on, Doctor, you're needed up at the Grange,' he said, the words tumbling out of him. 'There's been shooting, I saw them.'

The doctor stood. Now the moment had come he felt unsure, lost.

'Could we go tomorrow?' he said, his voice timid. 'I'm not sure I have everything I need.'

Birch was already opening the door.

'Better hurry, I reckon, doctor. Young Stephanie has been hurt, pretty bad too by the looks of it.'

'Where are we going, Birch?'

Birch took the doctor by the arm, picking up his bag, and pulled the door closed behind them. He set off towards the Grange, the doctor hurrying to catch up.

'Tell me what you saw, Birch,' he said. The doctor felt a bit more sure of himself now that the journey had begun, remembering the details of the duel that he had read.

'Don't reckon anything good will come of it, doctor. I saw them walking down, Stephanie and her brother and that Garrick. I thought it was a bit strange. They were all dressed up in costume, like old soldiers, with top hats and ribbons on their chest. It was a bit peculiar, if you ask me.'

They were emerging from the town now, the doctor slowing as they started up the hill towards Folly Lane, trees leaning in across the track, warning them away. 'She saw me, that Stephanie – told me to get lost, more or less. So I made out like I was off to get the cattle, but I stuck around to keep an eye out.'

A labourer was going to mow barley in the adjoining field and he, seeing three gentlemen come into that retired place, ran down and looked at them over the intervening hedge; when one of the party asked him roughly what he wanted there, and bade him mind his own business or they would shoot him.

The gold and ochre of the hedgerows shone with unusual clarity. Insects dipped in and out of the evening light. In the distance, the trees on the ridge of Folly Lane were stirring, as if in anticipation of a storm to come.

'I watched them in the copse, from the other side of the hedge,' Birch went on. 'That Garrick got them to stand there, back to back, like a duel, each of them holding one of these old-fashioned pistols. Deadly looking things. Then he starts counting, shouting out the numbers and they walk, like a couple of ghosts.'

'Did you see him load the pistols, Birch?'

He repeated the question. 'The pistols, Birch. Did you see him load them?'

Birch turned, not pausing as he strode up the lane. 'I saw him fiddling with them, doctor. Don't know if he was loading them. That important then, is it?'

The doctor knew enough about Birch to understand that he was aware of more than he let on. 'Yes, I suppose it might be,' he said.

'He starts calling out the numbers, and they start walking. Except young Stephanie – once he got to about number four she didn't move, seemed to be stuck there, staring ahead of her.

'As he was about to call out six, the boy turns, smooth as

anything, like he's a clockwork figure, and raises his pistol. Then he aims at his sister's back, calm as you like, just as she starts to turn, slowly, mind, as if she couldn't force her body round. And he pulls the trigger. Made an almighty noise, I can tell you. Big puff of smoke first, then a bang. Old gun it was too. Don't know where they got them. Must have been that Garrick feller.'

The doctor leaned into the hill, seeming to concentrate more on placing his feet one after another than on Birch's words.

'Then all hell broke loose. Mr Garrick started running around like a spring hare, yelling and laughing and whooping, the brother stood there like he'd been struck dumb, gun dangling from his arm, and Stephanie fell face first into the grass. The bullet had gone through her side, I reckon, though you'll see soon enough. Garrick was trying to turn her over but didn't seem to know where to put his hands, and Matthew was just frozen, like he'd been hypnotised or something. Then I started running down the hill to get you, reckoned it was the most use I could be.' They paused alongside a small shed, little more than a few sheets of black corrugated iron nailed haphazardly to some wooden poles. 'There's a scallet they keep in here we could take. Might come in useful.'

Birch and the doctor made their way down the hill, the sun fallen now behind the ridge above them, a chill settling on the air, the gloom deepening in the woods as he pushed the barrow, its wheels bouncing over the ruts in the path.

When they came to the copse, Garrick was sitting on the ground cradling Stephanie's head in his lap. He had opened her jacket to reveal a large red patch on her shirt. As they approached he held out his crimson palms to them as if seeking approval.

'I've tried to stop the bleeding, but it just seems to keep coming.'

The doctor knelt beside the girl and moved her head away from Garrick, placing it flat on the ground. She was breathing, her eyes open but listless.

'You've done well, Garrick,' he said quietly, years of practice dictating his actions, his voice calm in spite of the tremor of excitement running through him. He saw himself from above, a bird's eye view as he knelt beside the girl, opening his bag, taking out swabs, a syringe, pulling back the cloth of the shirt to reveal the wound. She was awake, aware that he was there. He touched the scar on her cheek. She stirred, a defiant look in her eyes. She opened her mouth to speak but nothing came out, her lips moving silently, as if she were miming. The doctor nodded, adopting his bedside manner, the one he knew would communicate reassurance to the patient, but she was already unconscious, her head lolling to the side.

He looked at the wound, the skin severed as if cut open by a serrated knife. His experience of gunshot wounds had been limited to textbooks, and the violence of it shocked him. The raw flesh pulsed before him, giving out its life. He turned the body, checking for an exit wound, and found the smaller neat hole he had expected. Taking gauze from his bag, he dressed the wound, wrapping a bandage around the limp body.

'We didn't bring a stretcher, did we?' he asked.

'We've got the wheelbarrow, Doctor,' Birch answered.

'Oh, yes, of course. How silly of me.'

Birch moved forward with the cart. Between the three of them they lifted her up and lay her down in the dirt and the dust of the barrow, her legs hanging over the end, mirroring the handles that Birch grasped as he prepared to push its load back up the hill.

'Where's the boy?' he said. The three men looked around them, as if aware for the first time that Matthew was absent.

The copse, stripped of the menace of the day, was bleak in the early evening, empty, the dim light flattening the ground.

'I thought it better he should take himself off, Dr Sweeting,' said Garrick. 'No point in him sticking around here. I told him to go far away, to forget any of it had ever happened, that it had just been a game.'

He stooped to pick up the valise. 'This is the only trace that he was here,' he said, opening the bag to reveal the red tunic that Matthew had worn. 'He put on the change of clothes and made his getaway, just as the story said.'

He took a step back and executed a curt bow to the doctor and Birch.

'And now it is my turn. Gentlemen, the second retires.'

Turning his back on them, he strode out of the copse, a strange figure with a top hat perched on his head. As the doctor watched him leave, he thought that despite his words Garrick seemed abnormally calm, satisfied even.

Sargeaunt retired to America, from whence, after some years, he came once to England, in secret, to see his aged father, whose only son he was; and then he returned to his melancholy exile where he died.

The Patient

The small procession made its way unnoticed along the lanes and avenues bordering the town. The girl had fallen in and out of consciousness, stirring occasionally, her eyes opening dull, unseeing, before closing again. From time to time words would come, mumbled, incoherent. Only once did she rouse herself, opening her eyes to look at the doctor, who was walking alongside the barrow.

'*Did I fire my pistol or not?*' she demanded, her voice deep, masculine.

'Yes, I believe you did,' the doctor replied.

Not pausing in his stride, Birch corrected him.

'No,' he said, 'you did not. I heard only one shot.'

'*Thank God.*'

She fell back, her eyes closed.

The rusty pistol had been allotted to Delmont; and was discharged after the duel, although not without difficulty.

Arriving at the doctor's house, Birch stopped the barrow at the front step and tipped it up, almost turning out Stephanie. Between them, they got her through the doorway and on to the bed the doctor used to examine patients, although he was not averse to using it himself now that the surgery had become quieter.

The ball had entered the left side and had come out at the chest. There was also a wound to the left arm.

This discovery caused great surprise, and a difficulty in understanding how it could have happened, unless he was left-handed, and had stood in a corresponding position with the left side to his antagonist.

'They were placed back to back?'

Birch stood in the doorway, his cap held in both hands before him. 'Yes,' he said, 'that's what I saw. If you don't mind, Doctor Sweeting, I'll be leaving. Don't reckon I'm cut out for this, shootings and the like.' He looked at the girl, pale in the harsh light of the surgery, breath barely disturbing her body. 'You know where to find me, Doctor.' He nodded, turned and went out of the door, closing it gently behind him.

The doctor looked at the figure lying on the bed, a blanket pulled over her. Stephanie was still wearing the army uniform, the heavy trousers and shirt, although they had removed the coat and her boots. She was watching him now, her cold eyes alighting on him when he came into her field of vision. He wanted to talk to her but doubted that she would be strong enough. He knew she could not stay in the surgery; someone would discover her and questions would be asked, why had he not stopped the duel when he had first learned of it, he could have easily alerted the authorities or even talked to the girl's mother. He would be ruined.

'Don't worry, Doctor.' The voice was firm, surprisingly measured. 'This was supposed to happen.' She swallowed, a dry click coming from her throat. 'Did Heazle run away?'

The doctor moved into her line of vision so that she could see him nod.

She smiled. Her body seemed to relax, as if exhaling.
'Good,' she said.

*

'*The wound is mortal, Doctor, I can feel it.*'

He looked at the pale figure lying on the bed. He was confused. He had imagined a scene such as this would be full of drama, of excitement. That was what he had hoped for, what he had pictured when the girl had first told him of the plan. But now he was stuck with another patient lying on the bed in his surgery. He felt let down. If Birch hadn't insisted, he told himself, he probably wouldn't have gone through with the whole charade.

The boy stirred again.

'*Doctor, I was shot in the act of turning round.*'

The boy spoke fluently. The doctor would remark later that it was as if he had rehearsed the speech, as if these were lines he had learned.

'*I forgive him.*'

The boy's mind wandered back to sleep, the body exhausted, fighting away the encroaching darkness.

A little later, although the doctor had lost track of the time, had not even looked at the clock, the boy stirred again, raising himself up on one elbow with great difficulty, grimacing and grunting at the pain.

'*Doctor, I'll tell you how it was.*'

Sweeting tried to calm him, telling him that it was all right, that he did not need to explain, but the boy continued.

'*We were placed back to back, and ordered by Sargeaunt to take six paces each, and then to fire. The word 'fire' was not given. I was shot in the back or at least I think so.*'

The doctor knew he should remember every word that the

young man said but was having trouble concentrating. The boy was rambling still, repeating himself, saying that he had not turned, that the command to fire had not been given.

It was light again when the doctor woke, a grey day emerging through the windows, the first signs of autumn pushing away the darkness of the night. In his sleep he had made a decision, a rare moment of clarity coming to him in his dreams. He couldn't possibly keep the boy here in his surgery any longer. There was too much risk involved. He might be struck off, and then what would happen to his pension, or his home? He would do what he should have done in the first place and take the boy to his mother. He would take the boy home – that would be best. His mother could care for him there, nurse him back to health, watch over her son. He would call Birch. He would help.

The Homecoming

The boy had heard the doctor move and listened as he picked up the phone in the hallway, the dial clicking back round on itself, the doctor's breathing harsh and uneven, as if struggling with the effort of using the telephone. He listened to the muffled conversation, fragments audible through the door, 'Yes, asleep... it will be best... his mother...'

Stephanie smiled to herself. She would go home, to the house of her father and her mother, the house that had seen so much, that knew so much. That would be where it would end. She was pleased with the way it had turned out, that Matthew had shot her and Garrick had given the orders, and that both had now fled. That much she had overheard during the night, had remembered from the journey to the doctor's. Now she would regain her place in the family, the adored child loved unquestioningly, the centre of their world.

Sargeaunt took off his regimentals, put on plain clothes; and, at nightfall, departed from his friends with such a stony look of desolation, as one of the dinner party, who saw it, could never forget. He rode on horseback and so escaped.

She imagined them clad in the clothing described on the

161

wanted poster. The second fleeing along the canal, the mist closing in on the dark figure, his coat-tails flapping behind him as he moved in haste from the scene of the crime. Heazle, her brother, pulling his beaver hat down, casting a shadow over his dark features as he was spirited away by the night, never to be seen or heard of again.

Birch came at the end of the day, once he had finished his duties to his animals. The doctor had started at the sound of his car, looking about him in alarm.

When the buzzer sounded, it was Birch who stood at the door, cap clutched in his hands.

'Reckon he'll be best in the back there, Doctor,' he said, nodding behind him at a dark blue Land Rover with a cab for the driver and an open bed behind, normally the preserve of bales of hay and Goodboy.

The doctor turned and went back into the room, Birch following. The boy was asleep, his breathing laboured but steady.

'We'll have to carry him,' the doctor whispered. 'He's too weak to walk.'

'I'll take him on my own, doctor,' Birch said. 'Only weighs about the same as a bale of hay.'

Birch scooped the figure into his arms, the lightness of the frame almost unbalancing the farmer, the doctor reaching an arm out to steady him.

He edged sideways out of the room, taking care not to knock the boy's feet as he carried him through the door and out to the waiting car, the doctor behind. Birch lay the figure in the bed of the vehicle, taking a rug stowed behind the seat and laying it over him.

'Should be alright, I would have thought,' he said, as much to himself as to the doctor. 'Not as if we're going very far.'

*

Stephanie awoke to rough hands moving her in the back of the truck, the pain again piercing through the shield of the drugs.

She followed the trees and the clouds as they traced her route slowly across the sky. The pain stabbed at her, even through the drugs the doctor had administered, and she gasped in shock each time they passed over a bump in the road. She wanted to cry out, to raise the alarm, tell them to slow down, that it was too fast, that they should stop for a while, that she only needed to rest. Instead she clamped her mouth shut, thin lips pressed together. She would not shout, she would not let them hear her pain. A soldier should not let his fellows see his suffering; she would do her utmost to retain what honour remained.

'Come on now, you're home.'

She felt Birch's broad arms lift her out of the truck and relaxed her body into him, letting the pain seep away, the smell of tar soap flooding into her nostrils.

The doctor moved ahead of them but before he could reach to knock on the door it opened to reveal Stephanie's mother.

'My word, Doctor, what a procession.' She smiled at the doctor, as if she had bumped into him at one of the fixtures on the town's social calendar. 'To what do I owe this honour?'

Stephanie struggled to keep her eyes open. Her mother was unrecognisable. She had tied her hair up and was wearing a bright summer dress.

The doctor gestured uselessly at the air before him, his arm flailing. Stephanie's mother stood and smiled, waiting for him to explain the motive for the unexpected house call, looking beyond him to Birch.

'I've brought your boy, Muriel,' he said, nodding behind him. 'We'd better get him in.'

She stood across the entrance, arms folded.

'We need to get him in,' Sweeting repeated. Birch started to move towards the house.

Stephanie's mother remained in the doorway, her smile fixed.

'I don't know what you mean, Doctor,' she said, 'my son is here. I hardly need another one.' She turned her head and shouted in a sing-song voice into the house – 'Matthew!' – then turned back to smile again at the doctor. The group stood, waiting, Stephanie's mother guarding the door, the doctor facing her, Birch bearing his load, Stephanie shivering in his arms.

'Here he is!'

Matthew appeared at the door, the book in one hand. He was wearing familiar Matthew clothes, grey, drab and shapeless. He came out tentatively and stood on the porch next to his mother. He stared wide eyed at the tableau arranged before him, Birch holding a shrouded figure, the doctor poised like a supplicant before them.

'I think I should go inside, Mother,' he said, his voice trembling. 'I don't feel very well, and I need to finish my book.'

He started to turn away but his mother positioned him directly in front of her.

'Now, darling,' she said, 'Doctor Sweeting said that he had brought my son back to me. I tried to tell him that you were here safe and sound, and that one was quite enough.' She laughed.

'Oh.' Matthew turned and smiled at the doctor which made him appear even more terrified. 'I don't think I'd like to have a brother very much, Doctor Sweeting.'

The doctor was flustered. He looked back at Birch, still holding the boy. 'It's Delmont,' he said. 'From the duel.'

The mother and son didn't move, she peering back at the

doctor with a superior air, Matthew staring fixedly at the ground. The doctor turned again and beckoned to Birch.

'Could you bring the boy here, Birch,' he said, his voice tentative.

Birch moved forwards as if he was bearing an offering.

'Here.'

He held the figure up to the woman, but she made no motion to inspect it. The doctor moved to Birch's side and pulled the blanket away from Stephanie's head, as if uncovering a corpse in a mortuary. A shock of mousey hair, hacked and unkempt, sticky with sweat, protruded over a girl's fragile face, its angular features disfigured by a livid welt running across one cheek, the cut violent against the pale skin. Stephanie's mother and brother both leaned forwards, craning their necks to catch a view of the boy. Then, as if moving with the swell of an unseen tide, they ebbed back, their movements followed by Stephanie's gaze.

'I'm awfully sorry, Doctor, but that's not my son. He doesn't look very well, but you are a doctor after all, so I suppose you must know what you're doing.' She ended the last words with a faint inflection, as if asking a question.

'He was injured,' he said, 'in the duel. He's lost a lot of blood.'

Mother and son both looked at the doctor.

'A duel?' she said. 'How preposterous.'

Birch spoke before the doctor could respond.

'Must have been a mistake, that's what I reckon. Someone gets something fixed in their minds and there's no knowing what might happen – get an idea about something and all of a sudden you've got yourself a situation.'

He turned, carrying the prostrate figure of the boy back to the Land Rover.

'Come on then, Doctor,' he said over his shoulder. 'Looks like we're in the wrong place.'

The doctor turned to Stephanie's mother. She regarded him with a distant look.

'Goodbye, Doctor,' she said, extending her hand to him. 'I'm sure we won't need to call on your services again, will we, Matthew?'

'No, Mother,' the boy mumbled and retreated inside the house.

She extracted her hand from the doctor's grasp and followed her son, the door closing softly behind them.

There was a rumble as the Land Rover coughed into life. Birch's ruddy face was mouthing something through the glass of the windscreen, a big hand beckoning.

The Admission

Sweeting told Birch where to take the boy, not looking the farmer in the eye as he said the name.

'Reckon it's a place she could be comfortable in for a while,' Birch said, as if to reassure the doctor. 'Used to be somewhere people would go to if they had nowhere else, or no one to turn to like. Not all of them in there are peculiar. Some are but others are just as regular as you and me, Doctor.' He paused, but the doctor seemed oblivious to his words.

'Take that Mr Garrick,' Birch continued. 'Think he belongs there, if you don't mind me saying. Very strange one he is, loitering around the town, dressed up to the nines, and then scampering here and there like he was still a kid.'

It was getting dark by the time they reached the asylum, the failing light shrouding the name carved into the gateposts. They drove up the long drive, the bright lights of the wards illuminating the lawns, casting stacks of perpendicular yellow across the grass, bars dark against the glass of the windows.

'Why, Birch, it's the asylum,' the doctor exclaimed. 'What are we doing here?'

Birch turned off the engine. 'For young Stephanie,' he said. 'You thought it would be best to bring her here.'

The doctor stared at him wide eyed, as if he didn't understand the language Birch was using.

'Your patient, Doctor, in the back,' Birch said, turning towards the figure laid out in the back of the Land Rover. 'We'd better get him in.'

'Oh God,' the doctor said. 'Why do I keep forgetting?' He slapped himself hard on the side of the head, exclaiming as he did so. 'Stupid, stupid, stupid fool.'

Birch waited for the tantrum to end. 'Do you want me to knock on the door, Doctor?'

'No, Birch, I'll do it. I can still do some things, you know.'

The doctor walked to the entrance and brought the heel of his palm down against the door. The thump echoed inside, followed by another and then another as he brought his hand down again, striking up a steady rhythm that did not abate until there was the sound of a key being turned in the lock. The door opened to reveal Mr Kirkbride in his grey overall, keys in one hand, a cigarette in his mouth.

'Can you not read the notice on the door?' he began, before recognising the doctor. 'Ah, Doctor Sweeting. Haven't seen you here for a long time.' He peered behind and took in Birch and the figure in his arms.

'Is that what I think it is, Doctor? A late admittance?' He blew a plume of smoke into the air, the three of them briefly following its progress from his mouth and out into the night.

'It's a young boy, Mr Kirkbride,' the doctor said. 'I think this is the best place for him, given the circumstances.'

Mr Kirkbride looked at the doctor, an old man with unkempt hair and stained clothes, like so many in the institution.

'Looks like you were in a rush to get here, doctor,' he said, forefinger and thumb extracting the cigarette from his mouth and casting it on to the ground with a flick. He ground it out with the ball of his foot, leaving a smudge of black across the step. 'I take it his will be one of our informal admittances, Doctor, given the circumstances.' He stood back to open the door wider and nodded to Birch. 'You'd best bring him in.'

They moved inside, into the green light of the hallway. There was a hush within, the only noise a distant mechanical whirring. A chemical smell hung heavy, almost liquid in the bright air.

Mr Kirkbride extracted a wheelchair from a row arranged by the door and held it for Birch. As the figure was placed in the chair, the blanket fell to reveal the shorn hair and the vivid scar carved into the pale face. Mr Kirkbride was about to set off along the corridor but stopped himself and turned back to the chair.

'Wait a minute,' he said, leaning in to the body slumped in the chair. 'I know this one.' He stood up straight, hitching his trousers around his waist. 'So she's finally moving in with us.' Swinging his keys, he set off along the corridor. 'This way, gentlemen,' he called out behind him, 'follow the blue line.'

*

The sound of Mr Kirkbride's keys had been in her dream, a jarring alarm warning her that a supervisor was coming and that she should be on her feet, pushing the buffer along the corridor and not languishing in the cupboard with Derek and Angela. The smell of the hospital had been in her dream too, the acrid combination of pharmaceuticals and disinfectant clinging to the back of her tongue. She felt groggy, the lines on the floor sweeping past in a blur.

Mr Kirkbride was sauntering ahead, whistling a tuneless theme. She tried to raise herself to see who was pushing her, but a shaft of pain seared through her side, causing her to gasp and sag back into the chair. She knew where she was now, recognised that this was not a dream, but that she was being pushed along a corridor in the asylum. She tried to move again, but found that she was strapped into the chair. She slumped back, watching the ceiling lights flick past, listening to Mr Kirkbride's whistling, the sound of voices intermittently echoing back at her from the walls.

Sweeting struggled to keep up. The walk was interminable, a giant circle circumnavigating the entire building. There was no one else in the corridor at this time of night. That had been one of the reasons they had come to the asylum, knowing that they would not be seen, that questions would not be asked about the boy's unusual attire or the nature of his injuries.

Mr Kirkbride stopped outside a door, indistinguishable from all the other doors they had passed in their orbit of the hospital. A brown plate set below the small square of reinforced glass bore the words: 'Anderson 1'.

Mr Kirkbride looked down at Stephanie, secure in the wheelchair.

'I can take her from here,' he said, putting a hand on the back of the wheelchair and manoeuvring it out of the control of Birch.

Selecting a pair of heavy keys, Mr Kirkbride unlocked first one lock and then a second before turning to Birch and the doctor.

'Just follow the blue line on your way out, gentlemen. Shouldn't take you too long.'

Mr Kirkbride turned his back on them and pulled the door open, pushing Stephanie into the ward.

'Welcome back, young lady,' he said, 'I thought we'd seen the last of you, but it just goes to show.'

He wheeled the chair along a corridor and stopped before another door, also with a double lock, which he unlocked before entering the room backwards, pulling the chair towards him. He manoeuvred it around to position Stephanie in the centre of the room.

'I think you'll be comfortable here, Stephanie.'

He had brought her to one of the isolation cells Derek had shown her when she had first come to the hospital. The floor and the walls were covered in the same soft material, stained and emitting a faint smell of urine. A solitary strip light ran the length of the room.

Mr Kirkbride undid the straps holding her into the chair and stood back.

'I told you to be careful playing with guns, did I not, lassie?'

She forced herself upright in the chair and stuck her chin out at him.

'I'm not a lassie, sir. My name is Delmont, Lieutenant Joseph Francis Delmont, of His Majesty's 82ⁿᵈ Regiment.'

Delmont slumped back in the chair again, the exertion of speaking in his military voice having drained him.

'Indeed, that's who you are,' Mr Kirkbride said. He moved towards the chair and pulled the slight figure upright.

'You need to stay here for a while,' he said. 'But I need the chair.'

He lowered her gently to the floor.

'I shall not die on a bed of honour.' She looked into his eyes, gripping the sleeve of his overall. *'I was not prepared to meet the shot of my adversary. I had not turned round.'*

Mr Kirkbride drew back, pulling his sleeve out of her surprisingly strong grasp. 'Ay, that's as may be,' he said. 'I'll be back in a wee while to see how you're getting on.' He closed the door behind him, the click of one lock followed by a second.

The Mother

Stephanie woke to find Mr Kirkbride looking down at her with Mrs Macleish alongside him, clipboard clasped in both hands.

'You said she'd end up back in here,' Mrs Macleish said, peering at the tiny figure lying on the floor.

'Aye, all that business about guns. I knew no good would come of it, Mrs Macleish. She says her name is Delmont, a soldier, 82nd Regiment apparently.'

'A soldier? Not a very hard-working soldier if I recall, Mr Kirkbride. I'm not sure I'd want her in my regiment.'

Mrs Macleish shuffled a step forward and inclined herself towards Stephanie.

'Are you all right there, lassie?' Her voice bellowed around the room, as if addressing someone on a distant shore.

'There's no need to shout, Mrs Macleish,' Mr Kirkbride interrupted. 'I don't think her hearing is impaired.'

'Oh, very well, I thank you for that Mr Kirkbride.' She returned her attention to Stephanie, adopting the gentle sing-song tone that she liked to use with the particularly vulnerable patients. 'Is there anything you'll be needing now?'

The figure stirred, the pale face presenting itself.

'*My name is Delmont, sir. I did not fire.*'

With that she gently lowered her face back to the floor.

Mr Kirkbride and Mrs Macleish exchanged a knowing look.

'There's no need for you to worry about the rights and the wrongs of it for now, lassie,' said Mrs Macleish. 'You just get some rest. Now, is there nae anything you want?'

Stephanie did not raise herself. She could see the two of them standing there before her like puffed-up guards. She swallowed and adopted a tragic voice. 'I'd just like my family,' she said, 'to see them for one last time.' She squeezed her eyes shut and a tear fell, the drop rolling along the length of the duellist's scar.

Mr Kirkbride and Mrs Macleish nodded in unison.

'Don't you worry yourself now,' said Mrs Macleish. 'I'm sure something can be arranged, just as soon as we get you settled in.'

When Stephanie next awoke she was lying in a hospital bed, liquid pulsing slowly through a tube snaking out of the back of her hand. A vase of flowers had been placed on a table, the crimson of the petals so intense that they cast a red shadow on to the wall. Her mother stood in the doorway wearing a tweed two-piece suit, as if she had been shopping at a smart department store in the town and had been suddenly called away.

'Hello, Mother,' Stephanie said. 'I knew you were going to come.'

Her mother looked around the room, as if she were inspecting it for dust.

'I really am most dreadfully sorry,' she said, 'but I'm not your mother.' She picked up the medical notes hanging off the end of the bed and began to read. 'You see, Joseph, I already have a son, and he's safe at home. That's quite enough for me, particularly since his father left and his sister seems to have

174

followed him. So I'm afraid that in your delirium you must be mistaken.'

Stephanie was barely listening. 'I knew you'd come,' she said, using her mother's hard voice. 'It's in the story.'

Her mother looked at her, a brittle smile fixed across her face. 'Story? I'm afraid, young man, that I don't know anything about a story. You asked to see me,' she said. 'Was there anything in particular that you wanted?'

Her mother seemed to be floating in the room. Stephanie squinted her eyes, but as hard as she did she could not get her mother to stay still. The lights were hurting, and even the effort of scrunching up her eyes caused her to wince in pain. She tried to swallow but could not. She felt so thirsty, her mouth so dry that she could not speak, her tongue swollen in her mouth.

She knew this part of the story. She had prepared for this.

'Give me something to drink, I am so thirsty, Mother. Nurse me.'

She tried to use her pleading voice, to remind her mother of the voice she had used as a little girl, but control was slipping away from her. She felt her eyes closing, the white of the strip lights replaced by the pink of her eyelids. Cold fingers touched her arm. Her mother was standing next to the bed, a paper cup in her hand.

'It's the last part, Mother,' she managed to say, her voice rasping in her throat. Her mother frowned, a look of worry crossing the stern face.

'Is this what you wanted?' Muriel asked.

Stephanie could see the pink liquid trembling inside the cup, as if a vibration was running through the room. She tried to lever herself up in the bed, but the pain arcing through her side was too much. She opened her mouth but no sound came. Her mother moved the cup towards her and she managed to nod her head, Yes, to the drink, Yes, to the end.

Her mother placed her hand behind her head and held her, the hand cool against the fever beating inside Stephanie. She could not remember her mother touching her in this way, caring for her, cradling her like a child. She looked up but her mother's grey eyes were concentrating on the cup of liquid, taking care not to spill it as she brought it to Stephanie's mouth.

'Drink,' she said, her voice gentle, soothing.

She touched the cup to Stephanie's mouth, parting her lips.

Stephanie felt the liquid settle first on her lips, then her tongue. She had no sense of a taste, merely relief. Her mother rested Stephanie's head back on the pillow, her eyes closed. She brushed the back of her fingers along the scar that scythed across the young face. Delmont did not flinch. The scar had healed over, had become a red slash, a feature that would evolve into a memento of a time and a story. The body lay still, at peace in the bed.

Epilogue

She could hear them, beyond, timid voices murmuring. It was a small audience, that she could tell: Mitzi was there, heels clacking harsh in the late summer sun, Derek weeping and snuffling. Mother was playing her part, although there was a shrillness to her voice, as if she were projecting for an unseen public. She could hear the doctor, too, his tread weary as he moved with the procession. There was no sign of Garrick.

They must be nearly at the churchyard. From here it would be a short walk across the car park, through the gate and along the alley, the cobbles uneven, causing her to sway, unsteady on her moorings. She had fashioned the box, this casket, herself, long hours in the attic, the plane clumsy in her hands, nails falling from blunted fingers. Her father would have been proud. She had not been convinced of its suitability; the lack of sturdiness, she had been sure, would cause its contents, herself, her body, to be spilled, sprawling on the road, her weapon tumbling out with her, the beaver hat toppling to the ground, tipping over and over, down the hill, forever down the hill, to be retrieved and placed once more so carefully on her limp body.

She was not sure who the bearers were. Birch would be one, and his brother, yet although the two of them were as strong as the beasts they tended there must be others. Her brother, perhaps. That would account for the lurch at each forward shuffle, the weakest corner sagging under the strain of the progress made. She could hear them breathing through the wood, each distinct in its inner noise, a sigh, a grunt, the imagined puffing of cheeks. Could there ever have been such a burden?

There was no light in this box, nothing for her to see herself by, to confirm her existence. Just her, in the dark, in her uniform, with its musty reek of battle and death.

They had stopped; the motion and the noises ceased. She hoped there would not be music. She had wanted neither song nor celebration. She had been careful to leave the words to be read over her. Her rites. Her story.

Unbound is the world's first crowdfunding publisher, established in 2011.

We believe that wonderful things can happen when you clear a path for people who share a passion. That's why we've built a platform that brings together readers and authors to crowdfund books they believe in – and give fresh ideas that don't fit the traditional mould the chance they deserve.

This book is in your hands because readers made it possible. Everyone who pledged their support is listed at the front of the book and below. Join them by visiting unbound.com and supporting a book today.

David Andrews
Nigel Baker
Peter Barnes
Ann-Margreth Bohl
June Briggs
Jonathan Carr
Lily Cheetham
Robert Eardley
Alejandro Gomez
David Gopnik

Josie Hardaker
Nicholas Johnson
Dan Kieran
A.B. Kyazze
Anna Lamb
James Layton
Frank Miles
John Mitchinson
Helen Moss
Carlo Navato

Justin Pollard
James Read
Eamon Somers
Sam Trounson

Bill Urbanski
John Wheatley
Reed Wilson